Take
My
Heart

Take My Heart

by Caz May

First Published 2022
Paperback ISBN 978-0-6488534-9-7

Published by Caz May

© Caz May 2020-2022
Cover image from iStock

To all my animal loving readers

Author's Preface

Hey lovely readers!

Please note this is an age gap romance.
This story is set in Australia, where the age of consent
is sixteen and at the beginning of the story the heroine is
seventeen, whilst the hero is twenty-nine.
Please do not comment on this in regard to the story
in reviews and such.

Caz May
xx

Playlist

Below is a sample of the playlist of songs for this story.
Check out the playlist for more!

Talking Body-Tove Lo
Sweet Disposition-The Temper Trap
Dakota-Stereophonics
Untouched-The Veronicas
I'm on fire-Bruce Springsteen

Also by Caz May

Secret Santa (A Christmas Rom-Com)

A Holiday Romance Duet

Bk 1-Take Flight

My Girl Duet

Bk 1-Not my Girl
Bk 2-Still my Girl

Always Only You Series

Bk 1-Roommates Don't Kiss & Tell
Bk 2-Friends Don't Say Goodbye
Bk 3-Feelings Don't Play Fair
Bk 4-Hearts Don't Steer Us Wrong

The Mackenney Family Saga

Bk 1-Country Secrets
Bk 2-Doctor Attraction
Bk 3-Unlawful Attachment

ix

Prologue

Madison

Wearing a beige wedding dress, I take each step of the lavish city church one by one, inhaling a deep breath to calm myself. Thoughts of whether I should even be there crash into my mind, but I shake them away trying to focus on not tripping.

All eyes are going to be on me, staring at me, wondering why I'm walking down the aisle by myself. My nerves are on edge when I push open the ornate double wooden doors.

Hesitating I take another deep breath in, telling myself to take another step, to walk through the arch in front of me.

You can do this Madi, marry him, and then all the pain will go away.

Exhaling the breath I've been holding in shakily I hitch up the skirt of my dress, grimacing at the itchy taffeta brushing my skin.

Why is this god forsaken dress itchy now?

It wasn't when I'd tried it on in the shop six months earlier. It wasn't when I was sure that marrying Knox Ellersan was what I wanted.

I can't help but let those thoughts invade my mind, wondering if I even still want Knox, if I still want to be his wife.

No doubt, Knox Ellersan is gorgeous, the son of the equally handsome Kieran Ellersan who owns Ellersan Enterprises, the biggest and most successful development company in Melbourne. He's made of money, but never throws it around like some rich boys do which was exactly what attracted me to him when we'd met at a bar a year to the day.

Granted, when I met him he hid who he was, telling me he was a university student studying to be a Veterinarian of all things. It had excited me that he was smart, as well as good looking and the conversation flowed between us like we'd known each other for years.

When meeting his parents, the realisation of who he was hit me hard and knowing he had money to his name excited me even more.I buttered them up, getting to them by trying to show them I was smitten with their only son.

Even I know that I'm the ultimate manipulator, and I'd wrapped Knox Ellersan around my little finger.

Now walking into a church to marry him, after what I'd done I'm not sure if I could face telling the world that I love him, whether I can say, 'I do' to all the happily ever after, death do us part bullshit.

Stepping under the arch, the sweet melodic music swells and the full church of hundreds of guests stand up as I start the walk down the aisle.

Take My Heart

Looking up I notice Knox at the altar, a sickly sweet smile plastered on his face seeing me—his bride—walking towards him. I try to hide the sigh that overwhelms me, taking slow steps and taking in how dapper Knox looks in a fitted black suit with a cherry red bowtie.

As I walk, the sobs and voices of the guests fill my ears, making the rushing blood sound intensify, the panic setting in.

Stopping dead halfway down the aisle I drop the skirt of the dress from my hands, smoothing it down in an effort to calm myself again, to try and focus on taking just one more step towards the man waiting for me at the altar.

He smiles at me, taking a deep breath in as though he knows exactly what is running through my mind and is about to chastise me for my long walk down the short aisle.

Again I hitch the skirt up, running at bolt neck speed out of the church, only stopping to drop the skirt when I crash through the double doors again.

My breathing is panicky, shallow as I stand on the top of the steps, looking around for a quick exit strategy. I need to get away, need to run away fast from Knox Ellersan and his perfect family, his perfect life that I know deep inside I don't deserve to be a part of.

Grinning, noticing the Rolls Royce wedding car parked on the curb outside the church gates I rush over. Peering

Caz May

in the windows, my heart hammers seeing the keys are in the ignition.

Hitching the skirt up to my knees, opening the creaky door I slide in, turning the ignition over. It grunts, the engine not so kindly giving me the finger.

"C'mon, seriously fucking start," I curse, turning the key ignition with such force I could have snapped the key in half.

The old engine roars to life and I clutch the steering wheel with white knuckled fingers as I slip the car away from the curb, driving off to face my demons in a wedding dress.

Knox

Seeing Madison walking down the aisle in her beige wedding dress, my heart is hammering in my chest. My eyes are glistening with tears as a mega smile crosses my face.

I can't believe the day is finally here, that I'm actually going to be marrying her in a matter of minutes.

I want to race down the short aisle, meet her in the middle, grab her around the waist to spin her in my arms as I kiss her plump lips.

But my heart stops when she hesitates, turning away from me and running straight out the doors she'd just entered through.

I look across the altar at my younger sister, putting my hands up in despair, mouthing, *'What do I do?'*

My sister points down the aisle, nodding at me to follow Madison. I stumble a little, running a hand through my mousy ash blonde locks as I rush down the aisle, aware of every eye in the church on me.

Once outside the double doors, I give myself a moment to breath, my hands on my knees when I sigh deeply. I can feel the tears dripping down my cheeks, these ones not happy like they were moments ago. My eyes lock on the church gates, noticing that the cherry red Rolls Royce is nowhere to be seen.

Caz May

I scoff at her gall, anger rising in his chest. Trying to calm myself I breathe in, slow deep breaths, in, out, in, out.

I'm shaken from my reverie when my sister comes up behind me, touching my arm softly so I turn towards her.

Once I'm facing her, she frowns seeing my tear stained cheeks. "I'm sorry Knox," she offers, with sincerity in her tone.

"Don't Piper ok? I..." I cut my words off, not wanting to even say the words in my mind. I'm angry at myself that I'd not seen this coming.

Piper reaches out to hug me, pulling me close. I sniff back another sob.

Pulling back from the hug, I look to my younger sister as though she knows the answer to every question running through my mind.

"Why didn't I know she was going to run?" I ask Piper, leaning against the railing for support.

Piper shakes her head at me reassuringly. "No one would have expected that Knox. Don't blame yourself."

"That's easier said than done," I snap back, cursing myself for being so abrupt with my sister who's only trying to show me she cares.

"I thought she loved me."

"Yeah me too, but Knox?"

"Yeah Piper?" I ask, giving her an incredulous, tell me now younger sister look.

I'd always been close with her since the day she was born. There may have been nine years between us, but I was besotted with her treating her like a princess until she decided that prissy dresses and Barbie dolls were not her thing.

Piper had always been worldly, seeming older than she is and just like me, she didn't let the Ellersan name define her.

Her next words show me that she knows far more about life and love than I give her credit for. She's far from naive and I'm a little angry at myself that I'd not been there for her as much in recent years.

"You deserve better than Madison," she suggests, a tiny smile at the corner of her mouth.

"How can you say that Piper? How do I deserve better than a beautiful woman?"

Piper smiles then, a sweet smile. "Because you're my brother Knox and she never appreciated what an amazing guy you are."

I smile back at her, wondering if she knows something I don't. We didn't keep secrets from each other when we were younger but since Madison had come into my life I'd drifted from my sister and regret for that is hitting me hard in the chest.

"Thanks Piper, can you tell Mum and Dad to let everyone know to enjoy the reception?"

"Yeah sure, you gonna be ok?" she asks, touching my arm lightly.

Caz May

"Yeah I just need some space to think about things," I reply, turning away to step down the concrete steps.

"Ok, I guess we'll see you back home later," Piper calls out to my back.

I lift a hand to wave to her, not turning my gaze to look at her. My heart is shattering inside my chest. Reaching the church gates, I stop, turning back to see Piper has gone inside.

Im not one to run away from my troubles, but that's exactly what I want to do as I walk out onto the streets of the city.

The church fades into the background as I dive my hands into my pockets, my black dress shoes hitting the pavement in a chorus. I try to think about what I loved about Madison and what made her want to run, but nothing is clear in my mind. Nothing is clear except the thoughts that my life is crumbling around me, shattering into hundreds of pieces, just like my heart.

Take My Heart

One

Knox

Three Months Earlier

*D*riving slowly into the coastal bush town of Lockgrove Bay, I look across at the passenger seat. Madison sits up in the seat of my white BMW coupe, clutching the seatbelt in her fist as though she's holding on for dear life.

I put a hand on her thigh, rubbing it comfortingly and asking, "Babe you ok?"

She looks at me, swallowing hard and swatting my hand away. "I'm fine Knox...I...I just don't why we're here."

Caz May

A deep laugh escapes my chest. "You know why we're here, Madi."

"Well, yes, but why can't we find somewhere in Melbourne?"

"Because I want to get as far away from my Father as possible and this opportunity seems to good to pass up," I reply, hiding my smile from her as I slide the car into a carpark in the sleepy main street.

Not saying another word Madison unlatches her seatbelt, getting out of the car.

Cutting the engine, I slide out of the car walking around the bonnet to take her hand in mine.

"Are you sure you're ok babe?"

"Yes, I just hate the country," she snaps, swatting a fly away with the hand not in mine.

"I'm sure it's not as bad as you think, Madi."

"Look around Knox, there's nothing here," she spits dropping my hand as she rushes off down the street.

I take a moment to look each way down the street, which I have to admit to myself is desperately quiet for just after midday on a Saturday. Madison turns to look back at me, disgust on her face that nothing appears to be open.

"Are you coming?" she snaps at me, beckoning me with a wave.

"Um...Madi. It's this way," I tell her, pointing in the opposite direction.

"Oh ok," she replies sheepishly, shuffling back towards me in her cherry red stilettos.

Together we walk a hundred or so metres down the street. My heart is pounding in my chest as I look at all the shop fronts. Some just appear to be closed for the day, some completely deserted with yellowing newspaper covering their windows like no one has set foot in them for years.

My eyes light up when I see the building I've driven into Lockgrove Bay for. It's in disrepair, the light sky blue paint peeling from around the door and wooden windows.

One window has a crack straight through the middle, right where the words, *'Lockgrove Bay Veterinary Clinic'* is, the letters yellow and peeling away.

Stepping up to the glass door, I peer inside taking in the dated appearance some of which is Posters on the white painted walls advertising pet care products that are curling at the edges, yellowing as well. They seem so old, for products I've never heard of.

On the front desk, an old phone with the circular dial sits proudly as though in a time warp. I laugh thinking about how long ago it was that I used one of them.

Madison grunts behind me and taking a step back I look at her worriedly, not liking her reaction.

"What a dump!" she grunts grabbing my hand and pulling me away.

"You can't seriously want to do this Knox?"

I feel a pang in my heart, looking back at the clinic and then to my fiancée'. I feel torn—between them both—my love for Madison but also wanting somewhere to start my Veterinary career away from my Father and my hatred of everything he wants in his life.

I can't be in the city anymore, pretending I'm happy, but I also want to marry Madison, and start our life together."Knox?" Madison asks, squeezing my hand.

"Sorry baby, I...I don't know...I"

She cuts me off, screeching, "Look at the place Knox. It's a dump! Let's just find somewhere to get a coffee and head home. This place is giving me the creeps."

I laugh at her silly, juvenile words.

"Don't be crazy Madison, what do you think is going to happen?" I question with another laugh. "There's no one around!"

"You don't know that Knox, a serial killer could be just around the corner," she suggests pulling me back towards the car, looking petrified like she's seen a guy wielding an ax chasing her.

"Yeah sure, Madi," I reply with a laugh again, pulling her close to kiss her softly.

She shrinks back from me, not returning my kiss. I can't help but wonder about how withdrawn she's been recently. I want to marry her desperately, but she seems so reluctant to want to be a part of my life if it doesn't involve the glitz and glamour of city life with money.

Take My Heart

Getting back in the car, I shut the door as Madison slides into the passenger seat.

"Let's go home," I say to her, reversing the car out onto the road. "And I'll put this ridiculous fantasy to the back of my mind ok?"

I say those words calmly, but I really don't want to let go. It's crazy but I'm already feeling more at home in Lockgrove Bay than I ever have in the city. There's an odd pull to this quaint, beachside country town that I can't shake, even as we start to drive away and it's in the rearview mirror.

Madi breaks my thoughts with a humph.

"Good, you can do so much better than this Knox," she says, a smile on her face that tells me her thoughts are only concerned with what's best for her.

"I'm not going to work for my Father, Madi!" I bellow gripping the steering wheel hard, my knuckles going white as the anger rises in my chest.

"I'm...it...will be good for you though, Knox."

"Don't you mean good for you baby? All the money you want, for whatever you want," I taunt her with an angry sneer.

"It will be good for us Knox. I love you. I just want what's best for us."

"Right, us," I snigger, under my breath taking one last look back in the rearview mirror with my heart falling in my chest as I continue driving out of the sleepy town.

Caz May

Madison means everything to me, despite her flaw for wanting finery in life and for her I'm willing to let go of my dream of becoming a Veterinarian, even though it's honestly the last thing I want to do. It feels as though I've wasted the last six years of my life at uni for veterinary medicine.

But for her I'm willing to do anything, anything except be my Father's lackey.

Two

Knox

Standing in the doorway of my Father's office I'm leaning on the hinges, shifting uncomfortably on the balls of my feet whilst I'm waiting impatiently for my Father to have time to speak to me.

I hate coming to the high-rise inner city building where 'Ellersan Enterprises' is, the whole building always feels stifling; suffocating.

My Father wants me to take over the family business but I want nothing to do with property development. It has never interested me, not in the slightest and all my

27   **Caz May**

Father cares about is money; money and where his next thick wad of cash was going to come from.

It's not that my upbringing was bad, I'd gotten everything I wanted, including my precious dog Mannix, who bless his sweet heart had now passed on. We'd lived in a lavish house in the Eastern suburbs and I'd gone to a prestigious school, getting good grades; excellent grades.

But despite that I'd never been the son my Father wanted, because I had no mind for business and that angered my money driven Father.

Watching my father now, I scrunch my face up in disgust when I gaze over my Father's desk, high with paperwork and a multitude of coffee cups.

Kieran Ellersan is madly shuffling the papers all over the desk, as he barks angrily to someone on the phone, "Of course I'm angry! I've lost a lot of money because of this deal."

Finally noticing me in the doorway, my Father holds up a finger towards me, making me scoff, ready to walk out the door when my Father speaks more calmly this time to the person on the other end of the line, "Sorry Donte, I have to go. My son is here."

Slamming the receiver down, my father sits in his burly white office chair, crossing his arms over his chest.

"Well, come in Knox. We need to talk," my Father says in a patronising tone, as though he's addressing an employee, not his own flesh and blood.

Take My Heart

I swallow the lump that has surfaced in his throat at my Father's words, the tone he used grating against my nerves. I feel like a child again, not like a grown twenty-nine year old man.

Pushing the sleeves of my shirt up to my elbows I cross the expansive office, sinking into the tub chair in front of the desk. I want to fire a thousand questions at my Father but just being in his presence in the huge office, with ceiling to floor glass windows makes me feel incredibly anxious, my tongue sticking to the roof of my mouth with invisible glue.

"Well, son," my Father starts, his tone a little less patronising. "Have you given any more thought to our previous conversation after your little trip?"

I can feel the sweat dripping down my forehead. I'd known this little talk was coming but it doesn't make me feel any less anxious about it, doesn't make me ready to tell my Father to stick his company up his own arse.

Again I swallow hard. "Well, um, yes and no Dad," I mutter, nervously bouncing my knees.

"What do you mean? Yes and no? That's not an answer Knox!" My Father bellows, standing up from his chair and pushing it back to the wall.

The crash it makes hitting the bricks shocks my ears. My Father has started pacing the room, with his hands clasped behind his back. He's clearly contemplating what to say next to me, his wayward son.

I break the uncomfortable silence, "I'm sorry Dad, but I...I don't want to work here in this prison."

He stops pacing, pressing his hands into the mahogany desk as his gaze locks on me, his eyes dark.

The bore of his gaze again makes me feel like a child who's in trouble for some wrongdoing. I shrink back into the chair, hoping it will swallow me whole so I can escape the room.

"Prison? What does that fucking mean?" My Father roars, almost choking on the swear word.

"You heard me Dad and you know exactly what I mean."

His eyes soften a little, his grip on the table easing.

"I'm not trapped here son, if that's what you're getting at."

I let out a laugh.

"Could have fooled me, Dad. You never were around much, so I...I just figured you were trapped in this prison of your own making."

"You have some gall Knox! I gave you everything you wanted, including that mangy mutt you loved so much."

I feel anger rise in my chest at his deliberate dig to hurt my feelings. He wasn't always so callous, but years of hard business dealings had desensitised him.

"That's not fair Dad! I loved Mannix, but I wanted your love too. I've never been good enough, not the son you wanted."

Take My Heart

"Well, you have a chance now Knox, to step up and become the man I know you can be."

I scoff at his words, wondering if he had even listened to the words I'd said just minutes earlier.

I stand up from the chair, turning back to my Father.

"I don't want to be that man. I don't want to be you, Daddy," I taunt, heading towards the still open door.

"Don't you dare walk out that door Knox José Ellersan! This conversation is not over!"

"Yes, it fucking is, Daddy," I taunt again, this time turning back to look at his reaction.

He's balled his hands into fists, the blood boiling inside him at my attitude. He'd never laid a hand on anyone but in that moment I can tell he wants to slap some sense into his first born.

"Knox, get back here! I said we weren't finished!"

Again I stand in the doorway, now feeling on top of the world for standing up to my Father. "And I said we were, oh and by the way I'm still marrying Madison despite the fact you didn't give me your blessing."

"Well, son, don't come to me for help when you're filing for divorce from the gold-digging whore. That girl is poison!"

"No worries Daddy," I sass. "I'll see at the wedding."

Walking out I hear his scream, his anger reaching breaking point as he crashes everything from his desk to the floor.

Three

Knox

Four months later (After the wedding that never happened)

Glancing up at the top floor window of my parents Eastern suburbs mansion, I take in a deep breath, exhaling hard and trying not to cry. I'd always been sensitive when it came to emotions, especially those regarding my Mother's feelings. She always tried to go with what I wanted, even if it meant going against my Father's wishes.

Take My Heart

My Mother is now looking down at me from the top floor window, her eyes clearly stained with tears as she watches me—her only son—loading the last of my belongings into the back of my white Mercedes. It's clear she's feeling a jumble of emotions, afraid that she'll never see me again.

I wave up at her, smiling wide to try and hold back my tears even more. They're stinging the corner of my eyes and opening the car door, as I slide inside I wipe my bare arm across my cheeks.

Listening to the 'crackle crunch' of the gravel driveway under the tyres as I drive away from my childhood home the tears fall harder down my cheeks. I don't dare look in the rear vision mirror, as I have a feeling my sister is now on the doorstep saying a silent goodbye to me. We'd always been close, despite our age difference. The thought of leaving my family home was heartbreaking enough when I was going to be married but now I feel empty, completely wretched. I would also be happy if I never saw my Father again in my life.

Turning out onto Toorak Road, I sigh wondering if I'm making the right choice in moving to the country. Lockgrove Bay isn't far from the city, but it's a completely different world and the beachside country town is like nothing I've ever experienced on our family holidays,

Caz May

when we did go on them as they were always to some overseas destination.

My mix of emotions as I drive through the city streets is making my heart pound, my mind racing with the possibilities that lie ahead.

I'm beyond happy that I'm finally going to be putting all my hard work at university to good use, but I'm also heartbroken from leaving home and from Madison ditching me at the altar.

My heart shattered in my chest the moment she ran back down the aisle of the church as though she couldn't get away from me fast enough. Piper's words outside the church about Madison not being good enough for me had been playing on my mind for months.

I can't help but wonder if there was something else that made her run away. I was willing to give up everything for her, including the dream I'm now driving towards. Her betrayal ran deep and trepidation is rising in my chest as I get closer to Lockgrove Bay.

Driving through the gumtrees on the way into Lockgrove Bay, my heart starts pounding, not able to truly believe I'm actually there. It's actually happening. Pulling up in the main street, outside the rundown vet clinic I notice how out of place my BMW looks amongst the ute's of the local's.

Take My Heart

A wide smile spread across my face looking at the clinic, the real estate agent standing by the door. Stepping out of the car, I will my feet to take steady steps up onto the footpath to greet her.

"Good arvo, Melanie," I say to her, extending a hand for her to shake.

She laughs softly, greeting me in return but not taking my hand. Instead she pats a hand against my back and pulls me against her chest in a hug.

I stiffen in her unwelcome embrace, the feel of her ample breasts against my chest making me feel a little repulsed.

I'd only spoken to her over the phone and seen pictures of her on the real estate website. She'd been friendly and courteous in our exchanges but her sudden want to touch me seems unprofessional.

"So are you ready to see inside Mr Ellersan?" she asks, returning to the courteous tone I'd been getting over the phone from her for the past few months, as though she'd sensed my unease.

"Yes, definitely ready, Melanie," I reply stepping closer to the glass front door when I add, "and please call me Knox. Mr Ellersan is my Father and I'd rather leave any thoughts of him back in the city."

When I swallow hard, she nods. "No problems, Knox."

I could have sworn there was excitement in her tone at calling me by my first name, as though that changed the tone of our relationship from professional to something

Caz May

else. I want nothing to do with women, at least for the time being.

The pain of Madison running out of my life is still too raw. I know I'm considered a good looking guy, often having had girls throwing themselves at me, but in the end, even if they find me attractive all they're usually after is my money and I'm tired of that.

I'd thought I'd found someone different in Madison, but as usual, she turned out exactly like all the other girlfriends I'd had before and now I'm ready for a fresh start.

Melanie fumbles with the ancient set of keys in her hands, finally finding the one that unlocks the glass door. Stepping inside she trips up a little in her stiletto heels, falling into my outstretched arms.

"Sorry, I forgot there was a step there." She smiles apologetically standing up straight and pushing her chest out as I follow her inside.

I want to scoff at her, but instead take a gulp to swallow the nasty words that come to mind, before I reply, "No worries Melanie."

Again she smiles, looking me up and down as though she's drinking me in, undressing me slowly with her hazel eyes. I'm wearing a white t-shirt and dark denim jeans with black sneakers peeking out the bottom.

Taking a deep breath she asks, "So would you like me to show you around?"

Take My Heart

I look at her as she fidgets with the keys in her hand, not eager to hand them over, but eager to spend more time with me.

I'm not up to playing her games, I don't need an attractive twenty-something-year-old showing me around my new vet clinic. The way she looks at me, her tongue darting out between her lips to moisten them every couple of seconds makes it clear that the thoughts in her mind are clearly unprofessional and not about showing me my new space; at all.

"Um thanks for the offer Melanie, but I'd actually like to get settled in and take a look around myself."

She swallows hard, huffing as though she's about to cry.

"Of course, no problems. I guess you'll need these," she says, handing me the keys before she turns back towards the door.

Taking the step down more cautiously she smiles back at me.

"I'll come by on Monday to finalise the paperwork."

"No problems, I'll see you then Melanie."

Closing the door behind her she doesn't say another word as she walks down the Main Street out of view.

I take a deep breath, looking around the vet clinic that is now mine. There's so much to do I have no idea where to even start.

Caz May

Walking down the light blue painted hallway I find a wooden door at the back. Gripping the handle I try to turn it, finding it's locked.

The keys in my hand all look the same, so I try a few until I find one that slips into the chamber and makes the door lock click when I turn it.

Opening the door, my eyes boggle at the sight before me. It's as though I've stepped into a completely different place from the vet clinic just outside the door behind me.

In front of me is an expansive living area, decked out in wood panelling that leads into a chef's kitchen with black appliances that give the whole space a worldly appearance.

On the other side of the room are three doors, all wooden.

Opening the first one I find a simple but still lavish guest room with floral bedding that reminds me of my Mum's decorating tastes. The next room is a small bathroom, with a toilet, rain shower and a gold claw footed bath next to a sink in the same gold appearance.

I can't quite believe this is now my home, it seems too good to be true and oddly well taken care of compared to the attached vet clinic. The last and final room is a master suite, with a huge king sized four poster bed proudly in the middle.

French doors lead out onto a courtyard with overgrown ivy and jasmine encroaching on the little cast iron chairs and table in the centre.

Take My Heart

Stepping into the room, I can't help but grin at my new home and flopping down on the bed I close my eyes, slipping into sleep with the keys to my life beside me on the purple doona.

Four

Knox

*O*ver the weekend, I spent countless hours in the vet clinic ripping the outdated posters down from the walls, stripping back the windows to the wood underneath and peeling the old linoleum back to reveal beautiful wood floors.

Getting to the last corner of linoleum I sigh in relief, wiping a hand across my sweaty brow before lifting my white cotton t-shirt over my head; slinging it over my shoulder.

I stop a moment to look back at my work, and out the front glass windows that I'd polished until they were

Take My Heart

pristine, ready for the cracked window to be replaced. I'd carefully scrapped off the peeling words, 'Lockgrove Bay Veterinary clinic' making a mental note to find replacements.

I feel content, looking around the clinic. It feels as though my hard work is going to pay off. I'm about to turn away to head back to the apartment for a much needed shower, when a grey haired woman steps up to glass door, peering in with eager curiosity.

Spotting me, she waves and gestures for me to open the door.

"Hi, Ma'am, can I help you?" I ask, sweetly.

"Oh sorry to bother you dear, I just heard the rumours around town that a new vet had arrived and I wanted to come by and see for myself."

I let out a little chuckle, both from the amount and the speed of the words that poured out of her mouth.

"Well, it's lovely to meet you ma'am, I'm Knox Ellersan." I hold out a hand for her to shake, that she doesn't shake. I wonder if all the women in town are so forward when she leans up to press a kiss to my cheek.

"Well, dear, it's lovely to meet you too. I'm Beverley and my husband Matthew and I own the local hardware just up the street." She points back down the main street smiling. "You be sure to come by and grab anything you need, on the house."

Caz May

"Thank you Beverley, that's very kind of you, but I'll be more than happy to pay for anything I need to get this place back on its feet."

"Oh aren't you a dear," she coos. I take a step back—leaning on the door—afraid that she's about to pinch my cheeks or run a hand down my bare chest.

"Anyway Beverley, I really must call it a night. I'll pop down later in the week for some supplies, you have a good night."

She turns to walk away, waving at me when I shut the door,

Heading down the hallway to the apartment, I sigh deeply. I'm desperate for a shower, to wash away the sweat from a hard day's work, and also the dirty feeling from having yet another Lockgrove Bay woman hit on me.

Once in the bathroom, I turn the shower water on to scorching hot before unbuckling the belt clinging onto the waistband of my dark worn at the knees jeans. Unbuttoning them and sliding the zip down they fall down my legs.

Exhaling I slide my tight Mitch Dowd boxers down my slim toned legs. I'd lost weight in the last couple of months and barely any of my clothes fit properly without a belt. Stepping under the cascading water of the rain shower, I make mental notes in my head about all the things I need to purchase to do up the clinic, as well as some new clothing items such as jeans and trackies. The weather, it now being late March is beginning to get

Take My Heart

cooler and by the seaside the nightly breezes are even more chilling.

I shiver just thinking about cold nights ahead whilst I run the musky soap over my skin, too tired to give myself any special attention down below my waist. I'm missing the touch of a woman, missing Madison even though I know that's idiotic.But thoughts of all the women of Lockgrove Bay wanting me makes me feel dirty.

My head is in a spin, and honestly all I really want is answers as to why she'd left me at the altar. I'm not likely to get those answers, and I'm not sure I'll be able to move on without knowing the truth.

The women of Lockgrove Bay so far seem as though they're more than willing to help me move on, but my heart isn't ready to fall for anyone else, even if my body is craving some action.

Caz May

Five

Dakota

Sipping my chocolate milkshake I'm trying to hold on to Benji's leash whilst he practically gallops like a horse down Main street in front of me. He's only small, a Pomski puppy, but he sure can move.

I'm falling all over the place, and have to dig the heels of my worn converse high tops into the concrete to bring us to a standstill.

Squealing, Benji stops, looking up at me with sad puppy dog eyes.

Take My Heart

Ruffling his head I coo at him, "Sorry, buddy. But you need to slow down."

He whimpers back, letting out an excited bark eager to get on with his walk through town.

Gulping down some more of my milkshake, we continue walking and my eyes are drawn to the Veterinary Clinic. It's been years since we've had a local vet, and I'm excited to not have to call on the old dufus from Sale. He has a walking stick and hobbles around coughing and spluttering as though he's about to die.

I'd also heard that this new vet was young and really good looking.Clutching Benji's leash tighter I wrap it around my hand as I step closer to the windows of the vet clinic to peer inside. The yellowed newspaper that covered the windows is now gone, the old sign is also gone, and the whole place is practically sparkling.

At first, he's not looking, his back to me as he's mopping the floor, sashaying his hips from side to side. All he's wearing are dark denim jeans, hung low on his trim waist. And I'm completely flabbergasted just from watching the muscles in his back flex as he works. I'm not one to find a guy's--man's--body hot or anything like that, but I can't stop staring. I should stop staring before he realises I'm there, but I can't move. I don't want to look away. I want him to see me. I want to see his face.

Time has stood still with me staring into the vet clinic, looking at him longingly, but also the vet clinic as well. I've been dreaming of the day it reopened, as I wanted to do

Caz May

an apprenticeship there, to become a vet nurse. The opportunity seemed like a pipe dream, but now it could be a possibility. I glance down at Benji for a moment, who is plonked on his butt, licking over his privates like he's not out in public. Silly puppy.

I'm about to chastise him, pull him away when my gaze is drawn back to the windows of the vet clinic. He turns around, spotting me and I gasp, suddenly breathless. I don't look anymore to see if he waves or anything, because holy fluff balls I've never seen a man so stunning. My back is now against the glass as I try to calm my breathing. Love, at first sight, is bollocks, but golly gosh I think i'm in love with the new vet. I need to meet him. Somehow. Look at me being all brazen. Who the heck am I?

Trying not to glance inside at the epitome of what can only be described as the most gorgeous of males, I scoop Benji up in my arms and run down the main street. I'd dropped my milkshake when my gaze fell upon the love of my life, and its soaked my flannel shirt. It's clinging to my body and the breeze is making my nipples pebble from the cold sensation. But I'm also feeling tingly in my knickers, from staring at him.

It feels dirty but exciting. I've never been interested in guys my own age. They've never given me this feeling--just from a look--even when they've tried to get with me countless times. I want the new vet to do dirty things to me. Gosh, who the heck am I?

Take My Heart

The thought of that gives me a head rush. And I put Benji down, telling myself to think of Logan trying to hump me on the dance floor at Drake's birthday party last year.

Yep, that worked. My knickers aren't on fire anymore. But I kinda want them to be, courtesy of the hunky new Veterinarian.

Six

Knox

It's been a crazy busy few weeks fixing up the clinic. I'd had new glass installed for the front window—and I'm doing some finishing touches now—smoothing the new signage to apply it to the window. From the inside, it's backwards, but knowing what it says kinda makes me feel giddy.

'Lockgrove Bay Veterinary Clinic. Dr Knox Ellersan DVM'.

It's so surreal to see my name on the window of the clinic that is now mine. Thankfully I'd gotten my hands on my trust fund, before dad could snatch it away and hold it over my head to work for him. I honestly can't think of anything worse than working for Kieran Ellersan, in the city and property development. The only good things to come out of being an Ellersan was the money I got to buy this place, and the business knowledge I'd gathered from being around my father growing up. I'm more than happy to leave him, and all the bad memories back in Melbourne, especially the whole being left at the altar by Madison part.

Women are seriously not worth my time, time that is precious now I have the clinic. And speaking of annoying women who aren't worth my time, Melanie is now standing outside the window, waving at me frantically. She gestures towards the locked door, and reluctantly I open it to her.

"Good afternoon, Melanie," I greet her, trying to sound more happy to see her than I am. Her blatant flirting when first meeting me a few weeks ago certainly rubbed me the wrong way.

"Hello, Doctor Ellersan," she practically purrs like a cat in heat. "I just came by to see how you're settling in."

Her hands run down my chest, lingering over my waistband and i'm thankful that I'm actually wearing a T-shirt.

"I'm settling in great, thanks Melanie," I say, trying to give her the hint that I really don't have time for her right now.

"Yes, it's looking lovely, and you're getting all sweaty and hot," she says all flirty.

Her almost childish words is making me annoyed. I push her out the door.

"Thanks for stopping by, but I'm busy," I say sternly, as she stumbles backwards on the step of the threshold.

She can't take no for an answer, standing in the doorway, her back against it. she keeps asking questions, "So is there a special someone back in the city? Do you have any family?" These questions are too personal which makes me even more annoyed and frustrated. She's my damn realtor, but is acting like a long lost friend.

"I'm not going to answer those questions, Melanie."

She giggles. Actually giggles like a school girl. And it's clear the only way I'm going to get her to leave is to leave myself.

Again I shove her a little, so she fully steps out the door.

"Are you going somewhere?" she asks, like she's not an intruder into my space and a stealer of my time.

Locking the door behind me—after making sure my keys were in my back pocket—I head down the main street, towards the hardware store. I wasn't planning on heading there right now, but it seems the only way to get rid of Melanie.

Take My Heart

She follows me down the street, the clip clop of her high heels on the concrete grating on my nerves. I just want her to bugger off.

Stopping dead outside the hardware store, I'm seriously angry that she's still by my side, considering we passed the real estate office on the way. Raising my voice I tell her, "Leave me alone, please Melanie. I'm busy, and I'm sure you are too."

Her expression drops, as though she's finally getting the message. She walks away without a word, but that doesn't make me feel any better, especially when Beverley is behind the counter all excited for a minute.

"Oh Knox, dear, lovely to see you."

"Hello, Beverley. Have those supplies come in?"

"Yes, dear," she replies, her smile fading when she adds, "You best be staying away from Miss Vizzolini, because of Dane. He's in the army."

I nod, ignoring her question by not dignifying it with a response. "The supplies, Beverley?" I remind her. And she nods, heading out the back to gather the special paint and other things I ordered to finish off the clinic. The grand reopening is only days away, and I still have so much to do.

When Beverly returns, I take the supplies and trudge awkwardly back to the clinic.

I spend the rest of the day doing the final things to make the clinic all brand new.

If only I could fix my heart so easily.

Caz May

Seven

Dakota

You'd think having older siblings that I'd have been to an engagement party, but Tempany and Ashton's is my first.

Ava—my best friend—is so excited to have a stepsister, but she has no idea what having siblings is like, except for her older brother Ashton. He protected her, warned her away from his best friend Ezekiel, but Ava fell in love with him anyway.

She'd always liked boys, didn't believe in cooties or anything like that. But really she's only ever had eyes for Zeke.

For me boys still have cooties—not really—but boys our age are idiots. I've had boys try to touch me or even try to kiss me and it repulses me.

These past couple of months though I've been thinking more about dirty things but I don't want to do those with a boy.

I want them with a man, and one man only—the hot new vet in town. He literally took my breath away and made me feel all tingly.

Ava has said Zeke makes her feel that way and whilst that's a little eww, it's kinda exciting. Speaking of my best friend and her boyfriend, she's currently sitting on his lap at the side of the dance floor, kissing him. They used to have to hide their relationship from Ashton but now they're officially together they aren't hiding it from anyone.

I really want to talk to her, as we've hardly even seen each other in the holidays and then only really at school otherwise. With Zeke home from uni in the city, she's spending most of her time with him.

I'm a loony toon, as coming out of the toilets I swear I see the new vet, but he wouldn't be here. He doesn't know Ashton and Tempany, so I highly doubt he'd be at their engagement party. I bump into Tempany then, as she's heading to the bathroom herself.

Hugging her I beam, "Congratulations, Tempany. I'm so happy for you."

"Thanks, Dakota. I'm so happy with Ashton."

"Yeah, you really love him, huh?"

She laughs, with a wide smile, her eyes catching his on the other side of the room.

"Yeah, I really love him. And i'm happy to have Ava as a sister too."

"Yeah, when's the wedding?" I ask, excitedly.

"Not until we finish uni. We want to be settled and stuff."

"Makes sense," I reply, nodding and smiling at her. I didn't really know Tempany that well before she got with Ashton, but she seems like a really nice girl. Really down to earth, sweet and kind. She's going to make a great teacher.

"Yeah, how're you going with school and stuff?" she asks me.

"Good," I reply, adding with a laugh, "I'd love to spend more time with my best friend though."

Tempany laughs. "Yeah, she's pretty much attached at the lips to Zeke."

I laugh again, pretending to wretch. "Makes me sick."

"Not boy crazy like your bestie?" Tempany chuckles.

"No, boys are not on my radar."

Take My Heart

"I felt that way until Ashton," she admits to me, giddily with that smile.

"Hmm, yeah," I mumble. "I should probably go congratulate him too. Catch you, later."

She gives me another hug and I head over to Ashton. He smiles when he sees me walking towards him.

"Hey, Kota," he greets me happily.

"Hi Ashy. Congrats on the engagement."

"Thanks, Kota. I still kinda can't believe it."

"Yeah, you being engaged is kinda crazy but Tempany is a sweetie."

"Yeah she is."

He can't wipe the grin off his face. He really loves her.

"And Zeke is a good guy for Ava," I say warily.

"He's like a brother to me, so yeah he is. And treats Ava well."

I nod, and he continues with a lighthearted laugh, "I just hate the pda in front of me."

"Yeah, they need a room."

"Don't say that, Kota," he jeers. "I know more than a brother should already."

"I bet," I reply, not sure what else to say.

I've known Ashton most of my life, since Ava and I met at kindy and were inseparable, but I'm still an awkward dufus around him. This is probably the longest conversation we've ever had and even though he's not a guy I'm interested in, in that way for so many reasons I can't talk to him.

Caz May

I can't talk to any guy my age--except for pleasantries--
and it makes me feel like a stupid five year old.

Ashton breaks the silence, "Anyway, nice to see you,
Dakota. I'm going to go spend some time with my family."

I nod. "Nice to see you too, Ashton. You haven't seen
my little brother around have you?"

"Not since earlier when he practically tackled me."

I laugh at that. My baby brother Nebraska—well six
year old brother—is going to be a footballer for sure when
he's older. He runs at everyone whether he knows them or
not, practically tackling them to the ground. It's cute, but
annoying.

"Ok thanks. Enjoy the rest of your night," I croon at
him and he gives me a kiss on the cheek that stupidly
makes me blush as he walks away.

I can't even contain myself when my best friend's
taken brother kisses my cheek. If I ever get to actually
meet the hot new vet I'll probably self combust from just
being near him, in the same room.

I need to grow some lady balls, get some country girl
sass. But even if I do pull on my big girl cowgirl boots I
won't be going for a guy my age.

Certified, horny idiots. They might as well be roosters.

My best friend is still busy with her boyfriend and even
though I want to talk to her, I'm going to leave her to her
kissing in public session and track down the only boy in my
life, my little brother.

Maybe I'll be a spinster, becoming the old woman who lives for animals. It doesn't seem like the worst idea, but I also love the idea of falling in love like in the Hallmark movies I watch on Friday nights with mum—when I'm not at Ava's—and I want to know what it would be like to be loved by a man. Not a boy, but a man like the hot vet.

Caz May

Eight

Knox

*I*t had been quite a feat to just put an ad in the local newspaper for help at the clinic. The old vet didn't have anyone work with him, nor a mobile phone.

I have no idea how he even ran things or saw clients without bookings and a phone when out in the community.

Take My Heart

The old Ute he'd had parked at the back of the clinic was a bucket, but it ran and that was good enough for me.

My Mercedes wasn't fit for call outs to farms, or near beach driving, to be honest, but I wasn't about to let that go yet, just in case the old Ute did give up the ghost.

Nervously I'm pacing the clinic, flipping through the applications for the vet nurse, and receptionist position. I can only afford one for the moment, having spent way more doing up the place than I thought I would.

I'm interviewing three people, two women and a guy. I'd love to employ the guy, but knowing luck one of the women will be the right fit. And I'm a little worried that I'll be stuck with an employee who wants more than just a job from me. All the women I've met so far in Lockgrove Bay—married or single—seem to want me, and that's not me being cocky or pretentious. They've all thrown themselves at me, in one or another and it really rubs me the wrong way.

Hence my obvious unease, for interviewing for staff. The first candidate comes in, wiping her feet on the mat at the door. She smiles at me, holding her hand out to greet me

Taking it she says, "Hello, I'm Andrea. I'm here for the pole dancing job."

Her tone is jovial and I instantly like her.

"Lovely to meet you Andrea, but are you sure you're in the right place?" I question with a smirk, and chuckle.

"Yes, Dr Ellersan. Gotta lighten the mood a little. I'm getting the vibe that you're a bit uptight about interviewing."

"You could say that. It's just the women in this town are so forward. Kinda scares me," I admit glancing down to her hands by her side. She's wearing an engagement ring.

Andrea nods, laughing. "Let me guess? Melanie?"

"Yeah," I affirm, laughing with my nod. "That woman won't let up."

Andrea laughs. "Yeah, her partner Dane left for the army a year or so ago now. The rumour mill about what really happened between them is rife around town."

"Oh, right. I'll definitely steer clear. She's not my type. I'd rather not be climbed like I'm a tree."

"Understandable, but being a vet here you might get the occasional wildlife call out and koala's climb trees."

"Well, Andrea. I appreciate the heads up, and honestly I'm already thinking you're the right fit for this job."

"That's wonderful," she says with a smile. She doesn't want to jump me, and I feel calm around her as though I've known her my whole life. I need a friend in this town.

"Would you like to have a look around?"

"That would be lovely."

I show her around the clinic, and she takes everything in, eagerly with a wide happy grin the whole time. When the interview time is up, and the next person comes in I show Andrea out, telling her I'll be in contact. The other two candidates haven't even been interviewed yet but I've made up for my mind. Andrea is perfect for the job.

After I've wrapped up the final interview, having one hundred percent decided that I'm going with Andrea, I'm locking the door when a red head woman appears at the door, waving frantically at me, and pointing down at the lock indicating to let her in.

Talking to Andrea about her has summoned the she devil and she's dressed the part in a skin tight short as hell red dress and red stilettos. She just needs horns and she'd have the perfect halloween outfit.

Scoffing, I open the door again, holding it as I stand against it.

"Hello, Melanie. How can I help you?" I mock, sarcasm lacing my voice.

"I just wanted to come along and see how you're settling in," she coos, emphasising the word come, rolling the words off her tongue in a sultry way that turns my stomach.

"I'm fine Melanie," I grunt at her, not really in the mood for her flirting. I should've just ignored her and left her standing there. But I'm a sucker for punishment.

"Just fine doesn't sound good, Knox." She practically murmurs my name, and I'm taken aback by her suddenly shifting closer to me, stepping up into my personal space.

She kisses me, hard taking my breath away, the words I wanted to say being swallowed up by her attack on my mouth. Her hands are unexpectedly all over me, touching the skin just under the waistband of my jeans. I'm kissing her back, but oh shit...*wait, what am I doing? Kissing her...seriously.*

I push her away, shoving my hands against her stomach and she stumbles out the door with shock painting her features. I shouldn't have done that. Accepting her kiss will only give her the wrong idea.

She stalks away, as I lock the door and run down the corridor to my apartment.

In the bathroom I strip off my clothes, and run a bath. Getting into the warm water, my mind wanders to the past, my history with women. Getting involved with any woman is not what I need right now. My heart still hurts from Madison's rejection and at the last moment. She tore out my heart at the altar, trampling on it, stomping on it honestly as she ran out of the church without looking back at me. And Melanie is exactly the same type of woman. One I don't need to get involved with, one who won't repair my shattered heart, but will make it unrepairable. My body is screaming for someone else, other than myself and my hand to touch it, but Melanie is not going to be that one to touch me. I won't survive that. And from what I've gathered she's taken, and I've already gone too far with letting her kiss me if she's taken by another man.

I need to focus on the opening of the clinic in a week, and shut down any feelings of the past. Focusing on the

Take My Heart

future—without women—in it is the only way forward. A fresh start in this beautiful town.

Caz May

Nine

Dakota

As usual for a Friday night, I'm sitting in a beanbag in the middle of my best friends bedroom. We're surrounded by snacks, popcorn, m&m's, marshmallows and fairy floss. Tonight is different though, as it's the night before Ava's eighteenth birthday. I'm not really one for parties, and I'm kinda dreading being at the

Take My Heart

party tomorrow as there will be alcohol, and practically two sips of anything alcoholic goes straight to my head. I'm definitely a Cadbury when it comes to drinking.

Swallowing a handful of fairy floss, I ask my bestie, "Are you ready for your present, A?"

"Of course I am Kota," she says with a soft smile. "But you honestly didn't have to get me anything."

"Don't be silly, Ava. It's your eighteenth birthday." Ava laughs, and I realise I just said that as Cher does in Clueless.

"Whatever," Ava jeers back, laughing hard.

I hear her sarcastic tone and laugh so hard I snort, which is fitting for the present I'm about to give her.

Handing her the huge gift bag, she beams as she pries it open to find I've wrapped the presents inside.

Firstly she takes out the large one, which is rectangular. The paper is covered in purple hearts, and Ava admires it for a moment before she tears it. Her eyes light up and her smile widens when she sees the familiar converse logo on the top of the box.

Frantically she opens the lid and takes out the white Winnie the Pooh and Piglet best friends custom converse. They have the cartoon friends hugging with the quote about being friends forever on them.

"Oh my god, Kota! These are stunning!"

"You like them?"

"Like them?" she questions, shaking her head.

"Yeah," I mutter, a little worried even though I probably shouldn't be.

"I don't like them. I love them!"

"Oh good," I mumble in reply. "There are more presents in the bag."

"I don't think anything could top these, Kota," she tells me taking out the other wrapped gifts. Next, she unwraps the besties t-shirt, which also has Winnie the Pooh and Piglet on it.

"Aww, Kota. It's so cute."

"Yeah, I thought it was too."

She can't stop smiling, taking out the other cute random stuff I got her, some makeup, and a small journal.

"Thank you, Kota. These are all amazing presents. I love you."

"No worries, A. I'm glad you like them, and I love you too." With my words, she launches across to my beanbag to hug me.

"You're the best bestie a girl could ask for."

"Back at you, A," I jeer smiling and then asking, "Are you excited about your party tomorrow night?"

"Yeah, so excited. I can't wait to see Zeke and see what he's gotten me for my birthday."

"Yeah, I bet."

"Probably something dirty," she says cheerily, biting down on her lip as she thinks about it.

"Yeah, your boyfriend is dirty."

Take My Heart

"I know. I love him so much though," she confesses. "I've missed him, especially fucking him." She laughs then and I feel myself blush.

"A!" I screech, a little taken aback by my friends' blatant confession. "You're just as dirty."

"You'd know if you'd lost your v, Kota."

"Yep, probably but not happening," I affirm shaking my head.

Ava smiles, knowingly. She knows me too well. "I know Kota. Saving it for the right person is worth it," she declares, adding a somber, "Trust me."

She shoves popcorn into her mouth after that to not say anything else. I want to say more, ask her some questions about sex but it doesn't seem like the right time.

"We should probably get some sleep, considering tomorrow night we'll be up super late," I say, yawning without warning.

"Yeah, I'm going to party all night," Ava admits with a loud laugh, standing up from the beanbag and stretching before heading over to her bed. I follow her and she pulls back the sheets so we can both get in. She grabs her teddy bear—that Zeke gave her for her sixteenth birthday—and cuddles it close to her chest, laying on her back next to me.

"Goodnight, Kota."

"Goodnight, Ava," I reply back, rolling onto my side to fall asleep, thinking about how different my best friend and I are. She's so much more experienced than me—in everything—and I wish I could be more like her. Maybe things will change before I'm eighteen but I'm not counting on that happening, as the only man I want doesn't know I exist.

Take My Heart

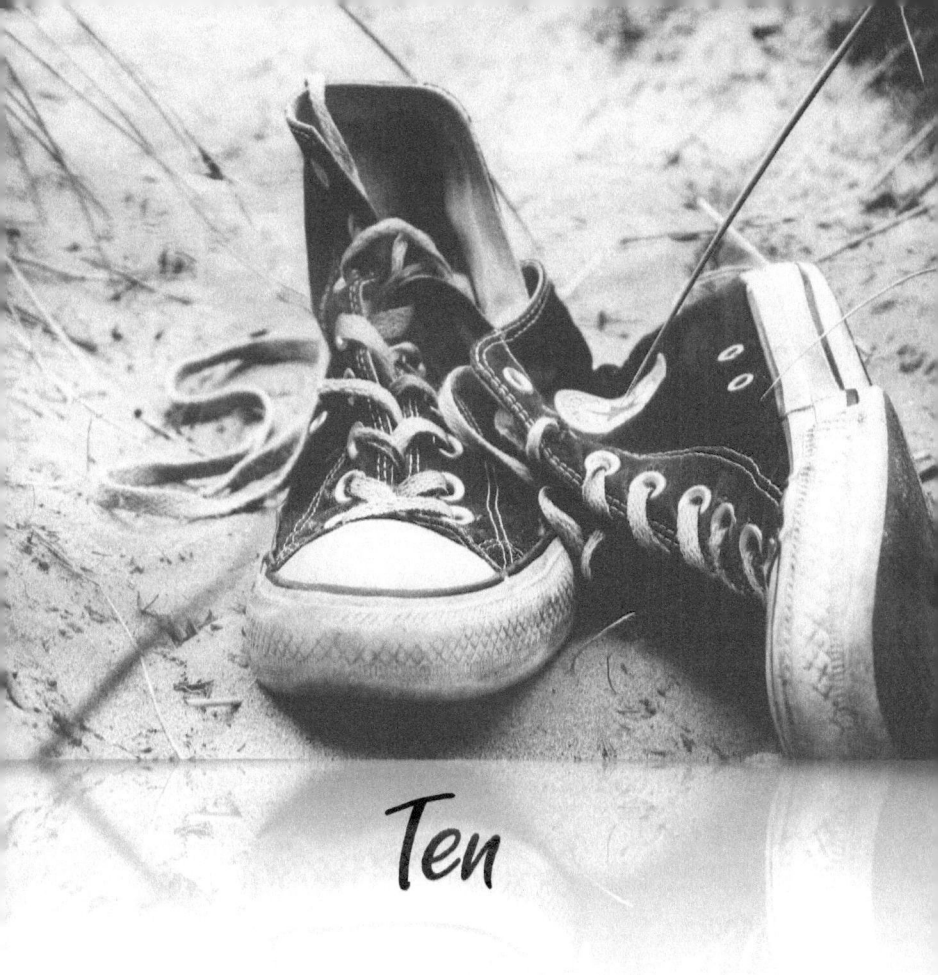

Ten

Dakota

The whole main street is abuzz with people, spilling out onto the road out the front of the vet clinic. The new vet has decorated the front windows with balloons and streamers and music is playing. Grabbing my best friends' arm, I'm dragging her through the crowd, eager to get to the front to get another glimpse of the hot new vet.

Caz May

I've not stopped thinking about him for weeks, ever since I first saw him through the window. I know he's older than me—significantly older—but that has me fascinated. And dirty thoughts have run through my mind—especially in bed at night-of what it would be like to be with him and kiss him.

There are so many people—seems like the whole town of Lockgrove Bay—is here to witness the re-opening of the vet clinic.

Reaching the front of the crowd—just in time to watch him stepping up to the door—with the ribbon between the doors, I'm panting for breath.

He's wearing a flannel shirt and tight dark denim jeans with cowboy boots on. He fits right in, in Lockgrove Bay—as though he belongs here—with me.

I can't stop staring at him, noticing that his name is on the window.

'Dr Knox Ellersan'.

I elbow Ava in the side, pointing at the window.

"His name is Knox," I voice when she looks at me, shrugging her shoulders.

"Good to know, Kota. Why're we here?"

"Because I want to be."

"You just wanted to see him," she teases me.

"So what if I do. He's really hot, A."

"Kota likes a man,"Ava jeers, when Dr Ellersan grunts into the microphone he's holding.

"Good arvo, everyone," he greets us with a wide smile.

Take My Heart

The crowd murmurs a collective greeting back, and Dr Ellersan continues, "Thank you all for coming out to celebrate with me, and Andrea today. Your support means the world and I hope you'll entrust me with the care of your beloved pets."

Some hollers and clapping reverberate through the crowd. And Andrea hands him some scissors that he cuts the ribbon with, announcing, "I declare The Lockgrove Bay Veterinary clinic officially open!"

The clapping continues, and some people cheer. I'm still staring at him, as people start to go up and introduce themselves, to chat to him.

Ava elbows me in the side, laughing.

"Aren't you going to go and say hi?" she teases, still laughing.

"No, I can't do that," I reply, blushing and nearly fainting when his eyes catch mine in the crowd. My heart skips in my chest with the way he can't stop looking at me for a moment, recollection as though he knows me.

I want to know him. I want to be brazen, and meet him officially, but with so many people around I'm edgy and nervous. I need to work out a way to meet him, to be alone with him.

And there really is only one way to do that. I need to visit the clinic with a patient. Ava glares at me, as I turn to leave the celebrations.

"Are we going?" she asks with an annoyed tone.

"Yeah," I mumble, scuffing my converse high tops on the road, looking down at the ground as I head back to the car.

"Kota, I'm sorry I teased you."

"It's ok, A. I'm probably just being silly about things."

I take one more look back to the clinic, and again my eyes catch Dr Ellersan's. A smile curves his lips, and getting in the car I wonder if that smile is for me, that he's feeling an attraction to me like I am to him. If he's getting the butterflies in his belly right now. It makes hundreds of thoughts tumble in my head, a thousand questions that I want to ask my best friend—and my mum—but I don't voice them.

Silly , fanciful Dakota needs to take a back seat. I don't need a boy, or a man.

Take My Heart

Eleven

Knox

After cutting the ribbon, I'm glancing around the crowd, my eyes catching with a young girl who's staring at me. Her gaze is locked on me, and by the way she's staring it feels like she knows me. As though this teenage girl can see right into my soul, my damaged heart even from across the crowd.

That very thought scares me, but excites me a little, a lot more than it should. Despite this uncertainty, I can't look away, sure I've seen her before. But I don't know

Caz May

many people in Lockgrove Bay yet, and if she's a local it's likely I haven't met her. It's confusing me, driving me crazy as I honestly can't work out where I know her from.

I'm also taken aback by her, how pretty she is. And I'm only getting a glimpse of her in the distance, in a crowd of people but this girl stands out like a beacon of light in a dark night. I'm feeling pulled towards her, by some invisible rope, but my feet are glued to the footpath. They're telling my mind to not go there, to not say anything to her, knowing she's young.

I'll probably never see her again, and that will certainly be a good thing with this attraction I'm feeling towards her. She honestly can't be more than fifteen, not legal for anything romantically inclined like my body is begging me for, and thinking about looking at her as she rushes away with her friend. It takes a hell of a lot of willpower to keep my feet planted on the footpath, to not rush after the pretty girl and introduce myself.

I'm an idiot for even thinking of doing that when I'm surrounded by people who are welcoming me into their town, putting trust in me to care for their pets, and not to take advantage of their youth.

I honestly don't even know who I am right now, thinking wicked thoughts about a teenage girl. A teenage girl who is younger than my sister Piper. I always shut down the silly crushes Piper's friends had on me growing up, especially the one friend Tabitha who practically jumped me and made me take her first kiss. I'd felt so

Take My Heart

disgusted by that—and with myself—I took three showers for days to scrub away the guilt and even scrubbed at my lips until they bled.

So now, I need to shut down any thoughts of young women--and women in general--as I don't need the guilt and the stress in my life.

I'm in Lockgrove Bay to fulfil my dream of being a Veterinarian, and I'm not going to do anything to jeopardise that. Failing in that would break my heart more than Madison leaving me at the altar.

Twelve

Dakota

Parking in the main street, a couple of doors down from the Vet clinic I get out of the car, grabbing the cat cage from the passenger seat. Hooking it over my arm, I tap the top.

"Calm down Minx. The new vet won't hurt you," I tell my cat who is miaowing as though she's screaming. Anyone would think something is really wrong with her,

Take My Heart

but she honestly just hates being confined to the cat cage and knows that being in that usually means a vet trip which she hates. The old vet was cruel. He didn't take much care in how he treated my pets, and I think Minx was scared of him in the end as she'd hiss at him, and bite him when he touched her. And Minx doesn't do that with anyone else, always the most affectionate cat who will purr on your lap all day whilst you stroke her plush soft fur.

Getting to the clinic I take a deep breath in, pushing the door open with my arm. The lady at the reception desk smiles at me, a smile that tells me she knows who I am. She does look familiar but I don't know her name.

Stepping up to the desk, I put the cat cage on the floor by my feet. It rocks a moment with Minx being crazy, but she settles when she realises the cage is no longer moving.

"Hi, I'm Dakota, and I have Minx here for her checkup and shots I think."

"Hello Dakota, it's lovely to see you. How're your parents?" she asks, and I squint at her name tag to try and place the familiarity.

"Um, they're good, Andrea. Lots happening on the farm as usual."

"I bet. It's great to have Dr Ellersan in town now."

"Yeah, I hope Minx likes him. She hated the old vet."

Andrea nods, laughing softly. "Lots of pets hated him, but I think they'll all fall in love with Dr Ellersan. He's wonderful."

I bite my lip to not say I'll probably fall in love with him too.

I already think he's the sexiest man I've ever seen, and that's without being anywhere near him, without meeting him. I'm nervous as a mouse right now, surprised I've even been able to hold a conversation with Andrea without mumbling.

"Take a seat, Dakota. Dr Ellersan will be out in a moment." With her words, she nods to the row of seats on the wall on the opposite side of the room. I pick up Minx's cage again, and she lets out a crying miaow.

"It's ok, Minx," I soothe, taking a seat and putting the cage in my lap with the door facing me so I can put my finger through for Minx to sniff. She instead licks it, her sandpaper tongue tickling my thumb.

The nervousness is still thrumming me, and I have to tell myself to calm down, to not bounce my knees in anxiousness because Minx is anxious too and she'll go flying across the room.

Barely a couple of minutes pass when I hear a deep, masculine voice, "Minx and Dakota?"

Gulping I stand up, gripping the handle of the cage. My knees feel weak, as I take in the gorgeous man in front of me. He's wearing a white lab coat with black and red paw prints all over it, and his dark jean clad legs show

Take My Heart

underneath it. They hug his hips and butt, and I try--and fail--to avert my eyes from his butt as he leads me down the corridor to a consult room.

It's warm and inviting, except for the cold examination table that makes Minx screech when Dr Ellersan takes her out of the cage.

"So, what's Minx in for today?"

"Just a checkup, Dr Ellersan," I say, batting my eyelids at him flirtatiously. "She might be sick, and need a doctors' special love."

My flirting is silly, but I want Dr Ellersan's special attention, his love. I want Dr Ellersan to do dirty things to me, right on the exam table I'm leaning against to keep myself upright. Just his voice makes me weak in the knees.

"Right, is her shots all up to date?" He seems to be stand offish, not looking at me as he asks the question.

"I don't know. She needs some love."

He doesn't say anything to that, so I add, "She likes you, Dr Ellersan."

And so do I.

"That's great, Dakota. Can we focus on the consult please?" he asks, a bit abruptly.

Huffing I reply, "She's up to date on her shots. But I wanted to bring her in to meet you."

"Is there anything you'd like me to do for you both today?"

'Um...kiss me,' I want to say, but I bite on my lip instead when Dr Ellersan looks right at me.

Caz May

"Her nails need to be cut," I tell him.

Giving me a nod, he crosses the room, turning his back at the cupboard along the wall. He grabs some small nail scissors and picks up Minx's paw to cut her nails. She hisses, her paw making contact with his arm, and scratching him.

He chuckles lightly, not fazed by my cat being vicious.

"If we're going to cut her nails, I'll need to give her a mild sedative. Is that ok?"

I nod, mumbling, "Yep." I don't know what else to say. I'm practically hyperventilating in this room being so close to the hottest man I've ever seen up close. I can see the beginnings of light brown stubble on his chin, and I'm wondering what it would feel like if I kissed his cheeks and his lips. His lips are a contradiction, the bottom one plump and protruding, the top thin and barely visible. I groan, wanting so badly to kiss him. I've never kissed anyone, I haven't wanted to kiss anyone, but I want to kiss Dr Ellersan more than I want to take another breath.

I'm so focused on staring at him, I don't realise the consult is over until he speaks.

"Great, well I guess that's all then," Dr Ellersan states, prodding Minx back into her cat cage, before opening the door to lead us out. I don't stop staring at him—completely smitten with the new vet—as I head out of the clinic.

My mind is in a spin, wondering how I can see Dr Ellersan again, without bringing in every pet I own into the

Take My Heart

clinic. I want him to treat me, focus his attention on me and not my pets anyway. I just have to think of a way to do that. I've booked Minx in for another appointment regardless, but I want Dr Ellersan alone.

Thirteen

Knox

*A*fter treating Minx—for absolutely nothing—I'm leaning on the counter, watching Dakota leaving the clinic clutching her slightly now out of it cat. Minx had been a little vicious—clearly not a fan of the Vet—and after cutting his nails, and getting a scratch on my arm I'd

Take My Heart

given him a mild light dose sedative. By the time she gets him home, he'll be back to his vicious self.

I must have a grin on my face, as I'm still staring after Dakota because Andrea laughs, joking, "She wants you."

I turn to glare at her, laughing myself with my elbows propped up on the high counter. "What makes you say that?" I question my vet nurse, intrigued but a little taken aback.

"She couldn't take her eyes off you," Andrea says cheekily. "And has booked for another consultation already for the same pet who clearly has nothing wrong."

Standing up straight, I reply sternly, "Right. Well, I'll have to put her in her place next time she's in."

I need to use the same voice with Dakota next time she's in, or I'm going to give the girl mixed signals.

Andrea scoffs, then replies with a chastising voice, "Or you could entertain the thought of someone else."

"Even if that was a possibility, she's what, fifteen?" I question Andrea, hoping to throw her off the topic.

She again laughs, replying with information, "No... Dakota is seventeen...maybe eighteen. Sweet girl, big family. They run one of the farms on the outskirts of town." It doesn't make me feel any better about my attraction to Dakota. Yes, I said it, I'm attracted to her, and she's seventeen. Like smack my head—repeatedly— emoji.

"Right," I stammer, licking my lips to calm myself down a little. "Well, I'm sure I'll be doing some consulting with a

Caz May

farming family." Andrea nods at my words, replying a quick, "yep." She's still glaring at me, and I add, "But nothing will happen with me and a girl so young. I might as well be her dad."

Cheekily, she slaps me on the arm. "You're not that old, Knox."

"Might as well be," I surmise, with a shake of my head. "I feel it sometimes, that's for sure."

"Yeah," she says nodding and then clarifying, "heartbreak ages us for sure. But you'll find your one." I don't reply, and she laughs again, before teasing, "Melanie seems interested."

I guffaw. "Yeah not going there either. That woman rubs me the wrong way."

We laugh together as Andrea gets up to leave. "You right to lock up tonight? It's date night with Tony," she informs me with a wide grin.

"Of course," I reply, stepping away from the desk as she heads out the front door. Locking the front door, and heading down the hallway to my apartment my mind wanders back to the consult, to Dakota's flirting—that I'm honestly not sure she even realised she was doing— and the spark I felt when I touched her. I wonder if she felt it too. It was intense, giving my whole body a shock, and that's scary—and wrong—because she's seventeen. Technically legal, but still wrong. I'm sure most people— especially in a small town like Lockgrove Bay—would

Take My Heart

frown upon a twenty-nine-year-old man being with a seventeen-year-old girl.

Stepping inside my apartment, I strip off my clothes, sniffing them for any evidence of Dakota's scent, and getting a waft of the fresh jasmine smell I groan and throw the clothes away from me, causing Toby to bark when they land on his head where he's sleeping on his bed.

"Sorry buddy," I tell him, crossing the room to pat him as he comes waddling towards me, wagging his tail. Petting his soft, thick black as night fur causes him to bark as though he's talking to me, and I reply, telling myself and Toby, "I need to ignore it, I know."

I need to ignore the spark, the attraction I feel to Dakota. Keep things strictly professional, or lose everything I'm starting to build in Lockgrove Bay. I don't want to be like my new dog, slinking back to the city with my tail between my legs, completely ashamed.

Caz May

Fourteen

Dakota

Again I'm over at Ava's. I practically live at her house, as I'm there just as much as I'm home.

Lying in her bed she's nearly crying into her pillow, clutching her teddy bear from Zeke to her chest.

"You miss him, A?"

Her gaze turns to me, lying beside her. "So much," she admits, sniffing back her tears.

Take My Heart

"What happened after you fought with Chasity at your party?"

That question makes her smile. "He took me upstairs, and gave me my presents."

Her grin is so wide, I know there's more she's not telling me. "Is that all?"

"No," she says with a cheeky laugh, "we had sex, and god, Kota it was so good. Zeke knows how to fuck."

I feel myself blushing at my best friends crude confession. I've been thinking more and more about sexual things, admittedly even googling porn in a private browser on my laptop in bed one night. I'd only typed in 'sex' and all sorts of images and videos came up that both shocked and excited me. Some were extreme and I snapped my laptop closed, nearly throwing it aside because it was so traumatising.

"Eww, A. I don't want to hear that."

"Have you ever looked up stuff?" my best friend asks causing me to gape at her as she's read my mind.

"Well, yeah. But it's still kinda eww. Some was really dirty."

Ava laughs at me. "Did it make you feel anything?"

"No, eww, A."

"You can talk to me about it, Kota."

"I know, A, but not right now."

"Ok, but I'm here for you Kota."

I nod, and Ava keeps talking. I'm sure she's saying something about what's going on with our friends, but I'm

Caz May

not even really listening. I've tuned out, my thoughts drifting to Dr Ellersan.

Ava questions me, "Kota are you even listening?" I shrug her off, sighing and she asks another question, "Kota, are you ok? Is something wrong?"

"No, just school and home stuff is getting to me."

"Oh ok, and yeah, school has been crazy," she replies with a nod.

"Yeah, I kinda should go home tonight, but I think I just heard thunder."

The loud rumble increases, and Ava jumps. "That's definitely thunder."

"Guess I have to stay the night. I hate driving in storms."

"Yeah, especially going to yours," Ava observes, rolling over onto her side, and clutching her teddy bear tighter.

"A, do you have another bear I could hold?" I ask, feeling as small as my voice, childlike and not at all like a seventeen year old girl thinking about having sex for the first time.

"Yeah, here," Ava says handing me her teddy bear, and grabbing the one sitting on her bedside drawers that's clutching a heart with eighteen on it.

We both sigh, holding the teddy bears close as we go to sleep. And I'm dreaming of being with Dr Ellersan and a way to see him again.

Take My Heart

Fifteen

Knox

I t's a quiet day in the clinic, and I let Andrea take a long lunch break. Whilst she's out, I'm sitting at the front desk, munching on my salad sandwich with my feet up on the desk.

Not really paying attention, I'm startled when the bell above the door chimes and Melanie comes in again, sauntering across the reception space with a sway of her

Caz May

hips. The dress she's wearing is skin tight, and red. She smiles at me, pursing her red painted lips when she coos all flirty, "Hello, Dr Ellersan. You all alone today?"

I gulp, swallowing the lump that's taken up residence in my throat. I don't talk down to any woman, but I honestly want to tell her to fuck right off, and take herself back to hell. I'm sure I can see horns sprouting on her head, through her mass of dark red hair. She steps closer to me, her heels click clacking across the floor. I'm tempted to piff my sandwich at her head, and watch the mayonnaise covered lettuce make a mess of her dress. That would stop her stupid, incessant flirting.

"Melanie," I grunt her name in annoyance. "I'm trying to eat my lunch, so is there something you need that's urgent?"

"Well, yes," she coos again, batting her eyelashes. "I'm having a party tonight and would love for you to come along."

Her eyes are pleading me, and of course that's the moment Andrea enters the clinic from her lunch break.

"Did I hear something about a party?" Andrea asks, eyeing me and then nodding to Melanie with a smirk on her face.

"Yes, I'm having a party tonight, and was inviting Dr Ellersan here."

"That's nice of you, Melanie," Andrea says, her tone mocking but Melanie doesn't notice.

Take My Heart

"So nice," I mumble under my breath, giving Andrea dagger eyes as I'm sure she's about to throw me under the bus.

"Does the party invite extend to all?" Andrea asks sweetly.

"Oh of course, you and Tony are so welcome," Melanie says all sweetly, and grating.

Andrea looks to me again, and I huff reluctantly agreeing to attend thanks to Andrea persisting with her eyes on me. It's the last thing I want to do, but I need to get back out there, and move on from Madison. Possibly even make some more friends, and get my name out there amongst the townsfolk.

At the party, I'm clutching a beer, slowly sipping it and trying to keep my distance from Melanie. That's futile as she quickly finds me, like I've got a beacon on my head.

"Dr Ellersan," she coos, stepping into my personal space and running a hand down my chest. "I'm so glad you made it."

"You have a nice place, and please call me Knox," I tell her, swallowing another gulp of beer so I don't say what's really on my mind.

"Thank you, Knox," she says with a smile, stepping even closer to me.

Caz May

My heart is pounding in my chest, being cornered by her. She's crushing me against the bannister of the staircase, and I can't even move an inch to escape and run up them. I'd jump out a second storey window to get away from Melanie's advances. The woman just doesn't take a hint.

Again I gulp down the final dregs of my beer, and pull the bottle away from my lips only to have Melanie right in my face, her lips on mine replacing the rim of the bottle with a kiss that makes me feel conflicted. On one hand, it's damn great to be kissing a woman, but on the other I'm not sure that kissing Melanie is a good idea. Giving in a moment my mind goes to wondering if I should just sleep with her to get some action. But when she tries to deepen the kiss thoughts of Dakota spring to my mind and I push Melanie away annoyed with myself for my momentarily lapse in judgement.

I shove the empty beer bottle into her hands stammering, "I um...have to go attend to some animals at the clinic."

It's an excuse to leave, and I'm sure Melanie knows I'm lying because of my hasty exit but I don't care.

Getting home I race into the bathroom, tearing my clothes off and getting into the shower. I feel dirty, covered in skanky woman. I shower off Melanie, rubbing soap all over my body, down to my dick that starts to harden as I stroke it. It's wrong but thoughts of Dakota surface in my mind, and closing my eyes I picture her on her knees in front of me. And instead of her hands on me, her sweet mouth is taking me in, swirling the tip of my aching dick with her tongue. The fantasy is so dirty, so deliciously wrong and forbidden I groan, coming all over the shower wall with her name a scream on my lips. I'm a bad man for thinking of Dakota that way, but it's a been a long time since any woman has gotten to me like she has. I need to do something about it, but I honestly have no idea what.

Sixteen

Dakota

It's damn freezing, and I pull down the sleeves of my hoodie over my hands, only leaving my fingertips bare so I can run them along on the shelves, whilst looking at makeup. I didn't really wear the stuff, but I wanted Dr Ellersan to really look at me—as a woman he wants—and not some crazy girl who only takes her animals to the clinic to see him.

Ava smirks at me, asking, "What's with you? You're acting weird."

"Nothing," I snap, giving her a scowl, and continuing, "I'm not acting weird. Can't a girl look at stuff?"

I pick up a mascara, wondering if you can choose a wrong type of mascara.

"Well, yeah," Ava says, grabbing a lipstick tester and opening it to test on her hand, her face contorting in disgust at the colour. "But since when are you interested in makeup?" she asks, picking up another lipstick.

"Since now," I snap, turning my back so she can't see my blush.

"Seriously, you're being a weirdo, Kota," she informs me, laughing.

I laugh then, turning back towards her, and touching the lacy g-string knickers she's holding.

"I'm not the one buying naughty knickers to send pictures of me wearing to my boyfriend," I tease with a laugh, surprised those words came out of my mouth.

"You try being in a long distance relationship with a guy like Zeke," Ava pleads, with a laugh, before her tone drops to a sadder one, "He's insatiable and every damn minute we're apart I miss him, but I'm afraid he'll fall into another girls arms."

I scoff at my best friend, shaking my head at her when I say assuredly, "That won't happen, A. Zeke is so in love with you, it's sickening."

Caz May

She gives me a smile then, thoughts of Zeke coming to her mind. He does really love her, and I think she's going to marry him.

"He's your endgame, I know it," I add with a reassuring smile.

"I know Kota," Ava replies softly, adding with a smirk, "But I still like to keep him interested, and phone sex is all we have right now with him at uni."

"Yeah," I reply, feeling my cheeks heat with a blush from thinking about what happens during a phone sex session. I've never touched myself down there before, but since meeting Dr Ellersan I've thought about it. Ava elbows me in the side.

"Kota, you're blushing."

"Well, yeah...um...eww, A. I was um...thinking."

"About phone sex?"

"Yeah, but I don't need to think about my bestie having sex."

"You're a prude, Kota. Phone sex is fun," Ava teases, sending my thoughts into a spin—wondering about what sex might be like with Dr Ellersan—as we head to the clothes section. I don't say anything to Ava about it, but I'm thinking of putting on some makeup, and getting Dr Ellersan to look at me with a dirty look. I want him to undress me with his eyes.

Oh gosh, who am I? And why am I about to buy lacy knickers?

Take My Heart

Seventeen

Knox

*C*hecking the front door of the vet clinic is locked I shiver with the cold setting in.

Thunderclaps reverberate outside, making the walls and glass of the windows shake causing the animals in the clinic to whimper.

Caz May

Padding back down the hallway towards my apartment I notice the door is ajar, and Toby is bounding towards me, his tail low as she whimpers, reaching me.

Ruffling the fur on his head, I assure him,"It's ok buddy, it's just a little thunder.

Toby whimpers more, as though he's asking for something. Since finding him wandering the yard behind the clinic—not long after I'd moved in—he'd warmed to me, almost instantly, and that gave me comfort that this—being a veterinarian—really was the right decision.

"Fine, you can sleep in my bed tonight," I tell him, heading back into the clinic with him following me.

Quickly, I check in on all the animals staying for the night in the clinic, making sure they're doing ok with the storm whilst being locked in their cages. I give them some food, treats and water, before heading into the apartment, keeping the door to the clinic open, to hear of any animals in distress during the night, just in case.

Getting into bed—wearing flannelette PJ pants but nothing else—I'm startled, sitting up in bed to listen closer, sure I can hear someone banging on the front door, screaming out, "Help me."

Toby's ears have pricked up, and he hangs back, curling up on the bed scared, as I get up and run to the front door of the vet clinic.

Reaching the door I flabbergasted to find Dakota standing at the door—teeth chattering, absolutely

Take My Heart

drenched from her head to her toes—holding a dog in her arms like a baby.

Unlocking the door I usher her inside, trying to keep my tone calm when I ask, "What's wrong Dakota."

She follows me inside as I close the door behind her, peering up at me with tears in her eyes.

Sobbing, she stammers, "He...he got...bitten by a... snake." She's panting too, clearly panicked and taking the dog from her arms I rush straight into the first treatment room.

Flicking on the light, I don't waste a moment, putting the almost lifeless dog on the metal bench. The dog is a small pomski puppy and his breathing is shallow, his eyes closed.

Dakota is right behind me, breathing hard as though she's trying to calm herself down. I can sense her panic as she steps into the room and right up behind me.

It's making me tense but also suddenly aware I'm half naked, as my dick stirs in my pj pants with Dakota's hands brushing against small of my back, at the waistband.

"Dakota, please step back I need to concentrate," I tell her, turning to face her, having to take a breath in to calm my racing pulse whilst looking at her when I ask, "can you pass me the stethoscope?"

Dakota searches around the room for it with her eyes darting around. I'm about to nod when she spots it on the bench and rushes over to get it, handing it to me. Our fingers brush, sending a tingle rushing up my arm.

Caz May

Disregarding that odd—and bad feeling indication of my attraction to a seventeen year old—I focus back on her dog, putting the stethoscope earpieces into my ears and holding the diaphragm against his barely moving chest to listen to his heartbeat. It's slow, faint but still there which despite his unconscious state is a good sign. Taking the stethoscope out of my ears, I turn back to Dakota who is leaning on the exam table, biting down on her lip, showing her anxiety.

"Dakota when did he get bitten?" I ask her calmly. Inside I'm panicking, hoping it's not too late.

She shakes her head, stammering, "I ...I don't know... maybe on dusk."

That makes me a little angry at her. It's near 7pm now, and every minute is crucial with a snake bite.

"Dakota that was hours ago," I bellow, squeezing the stethoscope in my hand to tame it down. "How come you didn't bring him in sooner?"

She starts to sob, again, muttering her words through her tears, "I only just found him...I...I sped here as it was."

Her demeanour breaks my heart, softening my anger a little.

"I'm sorry," I tell her with the calm tone in my voice again. "It's just a time critical thing," I continue, stepping closer to her—wanting to hug her—but instead I run my hand up her arm in a soothing gesture.

Again I feel the spark, clearing my throat to stop myself from saying something out of place. I have to step aside,

Take My Heart

using the exam table as a shield to hide the tent in my pants. I'm annoyed at myself for being attracted to her. She's seventeen. I'm twenty-nine. It can't happen, and I need to focus back on saving her puppy.

"Dakota, do you know what type of snake it was?" I ask her, hoping for good news.

She sobs a bit more, her breath hitching when she replies, "Maybe a brown. We've seen lots of them around."

My heart sinks with those words. Brown snakes are some of the most poisonous, and if they're still around this late in the year I'm going to have to get in more supplies.

"Ok, give me a minute," I reply heading to the door, adding, "keep him calm if he wakes up. I'll be right back."

Leaving the room I rush to the supply closest, to get the anti venom. With it in hand I grab the spare t-shirt I'd draped over the chair in the break room, shrugging it on as I return to the treatment room. Dakota won't be able to roam my body with her eyes anymore, and I'm both glad and upset about that.

It was nice to feel something—have the eyes of a woman, albeit a young woman—on me.

I definitely need to a find someone more my age, but I'm not sure if that's what I even want anymore. And that's wrong.

Caz May

Eighteen

Dakota

A few minutes later Dr Ellersan returns with the anti venom shot in between his fingers, ready to use on Benji.

I'm upset that he's put a t-shirt on as I was enjoying looking at his abs and his lightly tanned skin, with him just wearing PJ pants. I'd also wondered if he was wearing

Take My Heart

underwear—if men wear underwear under their pj pants at all, like the whole men in kilts thing.

Chastising myself for the dirty thoughts, I give him a smile when he smiles at me, making my insides flutter at the sight of his slight dimples.

He gathers Benji's fur at the neck, injecting the shot of anti venom in slowly and steadily. I'm in awe of this man in front of me, showing so much care to my dog, and not freaking out in the crazy situation.

"Is he gonna be ok?" I ask warily, as Benji still hasn't woken up.

"I can't promise anything, Dakota," Dr Ellersan replies, still with the calm tone. I'm honestly amazed by him, mesmerised by how perfect he is.

I'm sobbing again, and Dr Ellersan moves closer to me, causing my heart to start pounding.

"Ok...I...don't...want him to...to die," I stammer, wishing Dr Ellersan would make a move. To hug me, or even just touch me again. I don't know what it is about him that makes me feel this way, the self combustible, party in my knickers kinda way.

His words break my thoughts, "I don't think that's going to happen, but he will need to stay in the clinic tonight, so I can monitor him through the night."

Feeling anxious I shift on my feet, rocking back and forth on my heels as I say, "Dr Ellersan?"

He laughs, and it makes my stomach flip flop. He has a sexy laugh.

Caz May

"Please Dakota, can you call me Knox?"

"Ok," I reply with a nod, still really anxious. He makes me anxious, but I want to be around him, more than I ever have wanted to be around and close to boys my age.

There's tension between us—a silence—that has me on edge. Knox breaks it, "I think it would be best for you to stay here tonight, with this storm going on."

It feels weird to call him Knox, even just in my head.

"I can't...I...have nothing to wear," I stammer, adding a little more coherently, "and as you can see my clothes are drenched."

His eyes rake my body, with my wet t-shirt clinging to my chest and my tiny denim shorts. He gulps, awkwardly replying, "I'll get you something to wear after I settle Benji in a cage."

"Ok," I reply hesitantly as Knox starts to prepare to take Benji to a cage, picking up his still sleeping body from the treatment table. His breathing isn't as shallow, and his little eyes flutter open for a moment. I pat his head, following Knox towards the back of the vet clinic. Reaching the cages, he opens one to put Benji in, telling me, "Bathroom is the first left after you go through the wooden door at the end of the corridor."

I'm worried about leaving Benji, all alone in a small cage for the night, but it's the best place for him.

"Thank you," I mumble, walking down the corridor to the end.

My mind wanders as I head to his house, attached at the back of the clinic. I'm wondering if he's feeling the same as me, if he's gets the giddy tingling when we touch.

Stepping into the house I'm shocked when I see how expansive it is, wood everywhere, huge glass floor to ceiling windows and a log fireplace.

Conscious that I'm dripping wet still I follow his instructions and go into the bathroom. It's decked out beautifully with a spa in one corner and a walk in shower with crisp white tiles and beige stone bench with a square sink.

I peel off my wet clothes, my t-shirt, denim shorts, leaving my underwear on and toeing off my sneakers and wet socks.

Sighing, I yank the scrunchie out of my hair, shaking my long blonde hair loose when he knocks on the door, startling me, and causing my heart beat to quicken.

Caz May

Nineteen

Knox

Opening the door—after knocking—I hand Dakota some towels. She smiles at me, making my stomach flip with lust I shouldn't be feeling. She's only in knickers—her back to me—and that causes a gasp to escape my mouth. Her pale, but flushed skin is a sight to behold, slight curves of her hips that lead to a pert bum that her wet underwear is clinging to. She's gorgeous, and

Take My Heart

a bad part of me wants to step into the bathroom, and wrap my arms around her, pulling the wet underwear off her sexy body. I have to look at the floor as it is, to not glance at the mirror to get a glimpse of her tits that she's trying to cover with her hands.

"Thank you," she mutters, locking eyes with me and softly adding, "for the towels."

"No worries, take your time," I tell her grabbing her clothes from the floor. "I'll put these in the dryer for you."

She nods softly, and heading out to the laundry I fight with myself about going back into the bathroom, but I shake the thoughts aside, reminding myself she's too young for me.

My body isn't getting that damn memo, because I can't help the stir in my pants thinking about her in the shower, washing her sexy, fit body as I shove her wet clothes in the dryer. They smell like eucalyptus and the sweetness of rain, and inhaling that scent makes the tent in my pants throb. I have a problem.

Only a few minutes pass and she comes out of the bathroom, with only the towel wrapped around her body —tucked in at the top—and I admire her again.

Damn, she's gorgeous.

So not my type, but her sweet, innocent look, and the fact she looks nothing like Madison is sending me into a spin.

I've been pacing the room, waiting for her like a creeper, and I have to say something or I'm going to do something stupid. Stupid like run over to scoop her into my arms, and take her to my bed, to worship her sexy body all night.

Fuck! What the hell am I thinking? She's seventeen Knox. Seventeen.

I do take a step closer to her, towards the guest room, informing her as calmly as I can, "Your clothes are in the dryer. They'll be awhile." My voice comes out all husky, and I hope she doesn't realise that I'm finding it incredibly fucking difficult to keep my dick tame right now.

"That's ok," she says, flirtation in her voice, tugging on the top hem of the towel. I lick my lips, secretly hoping it slips, and chastising myself for that very naughty thought when I say, still huskily, "You're only in a towel, Dakota."

"I know," she replies, giggly. "And I'm not wearing my underwear now either."

I gulp. Oh fuck!

"Yep," I reply, swallowing the lump in my throat. "I'll get you some clothes."

She nods at me, seeming to be excited about wearing my clothes. And heading to my bedroom I'm trying to keep my want for her in check, because damn seeing her in my clothes that will be too big for her is going to be a sight. A sexy as sin—tempting—sight.

Going to walk past her, to my bedroom, like an idiot, I end up stumbling on my own feet, pushing her against the wall. Her breathing is loud, coming out in panting slow breaths. She's clearly aroused, and I'm so tempted—so fucking tempted—to slide my hand under the towel, up her thighs, to the apex between her legs.

I put my forehead to hers. "Dakota," I murmur her name, so close to her lips my breath against them makes her gasp.

"Are you going to kiss me?" she asks, raspy and almost begging me.

I pull back, steadying myself on the wall with a raised hand, and I shake my head, fighting with myself to say the words, "No...we can't."

Her eyes—deep eucalyptus green eyes—lock on me, and she murmurs, "I want you to, Knox."

I slam my hand against the wall, groaning from frustration. How she said my name, drawing it out into multiple syllables. It sounds unbelievably sexy. And I groan again, forcing myself to reply, "I can't Dakota. You're seventeen."

"So?" she questions with a pout that's so sweetly sexy I want to give in, curse the fact she's seventeen. "I don't want a boy."

I fully pull back then, not wanting to hear her say anything else because I'll give in—completely—and I can't be tainting my new reputation in Lockgrove Bay by getting with a school girl. Grunting, I step aside to go into my bedroom. Quickly I grab a flannel shirt, and bringing it out to her I throw it at her.

Caz May

She catches it and says, "Thank you, Knox."

It's all buttoned up and she slips it over her head. It reaches mid thigh, and she reaches through the collar, untucking the towel, letting it fall to the floor at her feet.

Fuck! I groan again, stumbling on my feet as I give her a smile, and say, "Goodnight, Dakota. Sleep well."

"Goodnight, Knox," she purrs, making my dick stir as I head into my bedroom.

I'm in for a sleepless night with my hand in my pj pants, stroking my dick whilst I think of her in the next room, wondering if she's doing the same.

Twenty

Knox

*W*ith a smirk, Andrea hands me a brief of the house call I'm heading out to. It's for a horse, at one of the farms on the outskirts of town.

I get into the beaten-down old ute—that belonged to the previous vet—and securing my phone to the suction cup holder I punch the address details into google maps and set off out of town.

Caz May

Watching the streetscape change from beach to bushland brings a smile to my face. Lockgrove Bay is such a pretty place, and now, even months down the road I'm still amazed that I'm here, living my dream. Being a country vet is so much more than I could ever have hoped for—this—going to a house call for a horse seems so much more rewarding than treating kids guinea pigs in a city practice.

I've always loved horses, having gone—much to my father's objection—to a riding school in the city. That first encounter, when I fell off the most placid of horses and was nudged by him as if to say I'm sorry made me fall in love with animals. I hid that love from my father for years, until I went to university, and now it's all coming full circle.

I'm hit with a moment of panic when the GPS tells me to turn off down a dirt road, that looks like it leads nowhere. I've heard of people following map directions and driving off cliffs. That seems like something likely in Lockgrove Bay, but I tamp the fear down as this far out of the town—which is closer to the beach—I can no longer smell the salty air from the waves. It's been replaced by eucalyptus and wet soil. The first of which makes me think of Dakota, and my mind wanders a little to our near kiss a few weeks back. She hasn't been in to the clinic with any of her animals since, and I'm a little worried about that. She's been on my mind constantly though, especially at night when I've not been able to keep my hands off my dick, coming as I've jerked off thinking about all the things

Take My Heart

I want to do her, that I have no business doing with a seventeen-year-old. I shouldn't even be thinking those thoughts about her.

Shaking the dirty thoughts aside, I squint at the sign when I pull up to an open gate. It says, *'Bay Meadows'* and underneath in smaller writing it says, *'Neelson'.* That seems like a familiar name, but driving through the gate I can't place the name.

The driveway is long, and I pass a couple of fields with sheep, and cattle and horses before I get to a barn, and long weather-worn farmhouse. I'm getting out of the ute, reaching over into the tray to grab my kit when I hear a voice behind me, "Hello, Dr Ellersan."

I drop the kit back into the tray, it clamours against the metal, spilling everywhere when I turn to face Dakota standing right in my personal space.

Oh shit...you've got to be kidding me.

No wonder Andrea was smirking at me when she handed me the brief. The bitch knew. And I'm going to give her grief for not spilling that little detail when I get back to the clinic.

"Oh, hello, Dakota," I say sternly, trying to be professional, which is a feat when she's looking stunning in light denim jeans so tight they're a second skin, tight enough to show every sexy curve of her body. And a billowy blouse that's clinging to her tits one minute and not the next. Seeing her again sends my body into overdrive with lustful thoughts. And I have to remind myself, that one, I'm here to do my job, and two, she's seventeen.

"I didn't realise this was your family farm," I confess, smiling to tamp down my anger, and lust.

"Yeah, been in my family for years now. And when Chesney came down unwell I had no choice to call you out here."

"Well, I'm here," I say with a nod. "Lead the way."

She hesitates, as though she's going to take my hand. But I don't let her make that contact. I won't be responsible for my actions if we touch.

Again I grab my kit out of the tray of the ute and follow Dakota towards the barns opposite. She's skipping along, and I notice the ornate boots she's wearing over her jeans. Dakota is the epitome of a country girl, sweet, but a little sassy.

Once inside the horse barn, she stops in front of a stall, smiling wide as she grabs a saddle and blanket.

"Hey, Chessie, boy," she cajoles. "The nice vet is here to meet you." Her horse whinnies, tipping his head as she strokes his face from his mane to his mouth, down the white strip of hair.

I step a little closer, eyeing the horse who appears to be in fine form.

"So, Dakota, what's ailing Chesney currently?" I question in a patronising tone.

Take My Heart

She laughs, all sassy and blushes when she replies, "Oh nothing. I just wanted you to meet him, and come riding with me."

I scoff, angrily, really pissed off with her for making me come all the way out here when there's nothing wrong with her horse. It seems as though she's trying to seduce me in territory that she's comfortable with.

"Seriously, Dakota. I came all the way out here, for nothing." I hate that my tone is angry and her face falls.

"I'm sorry, I just wanted to see you again. And…"

"And what, Dakota?"

She blushes this time, biting down on her lip as she mutters, "To go riding with you."

"I honestly don't have the time Dakota. I'm sure there are other animals back at the clinic that actually need a vet right now."

She shakes her head, smirking, and that annoys me, as well as excites me because her sassy side is so damn sexy.

"No, I told Andrea to clear your schedule for the arvo," she admits, stepping into the stall and starting to saddle up Chesney.

I'm annoyed at her, for doing that without asking me, but with the day mine seeing the Neelson farm doesn't seem like a horrible idea at all. "Right, well, I'm just going to go take my kit back to the Ute, and grab my hat."

Dakota calls out, "Ok, I'll be waiting Dr Ellersan." I want to correct her again, tell her to call me Knox again, but I brush it off, for now, heading back to the Ute quickly.

Ten minutes later I'm back at the barn. Dakota has Chesney saddled up and ready, holding his reins in her hand.

"Ready to go for a ride around the farm?" She asks with a sweet innocence in her voice.

"I guess. Where's my horse?"

Dakota giggles. "None of our horses are suitable for inexperienced riders."

"Oh, right. Will Chesney be alright with both of us riding him?"

"Yes Dr Ellersan, he's a stock horse. Strong as they come."

"Right, and please, Dakota, can you call me Knox?"

She smiles wide then, stepping aside, ready to climb into the saddle.

"Ok," she says, smiling. "Knox."

She climbs into the saddle, and pats Chesney's hind, telling me, "Climb on up, Knox and hang on tight."

Awkwardly I use the stirrups, and the strong body of Chesney to hoist myself up onto his back behind Dakota.

She clears her throat. "I told you to hold on, Knox."

I nod—even though she won't see with her back to me —and I wrap my arms around her tiny waist.

Oh holy hell! I'm touching her. I should let go, but I need to hang on and she's hitched the reins up with a 'cluck-cluck' command and Chesney has started to slowly trot out of the barn.

Take My Heart

She gives Chesney more commands, and he starts to canter as we head around the paddocks with Dakota telling me all sorts of things about their farm. I'm honestly not really listening, too wrapt up with the conflicting thoughts in my head about how wrong this is. Her intentions could be innocent, but every moment we spend together gives me a completely different idea. Dakota flirts with me, badly but she does and even though I know I shouldn't enjoy it, I do.

Something startles Chesney, and he stops suddenly. Panicking I let my arms loosen from Dakota's waist and as the horses' hooves skid in the mud I slide backwards over his rump. Trying to stop myself from falling I grip his tail in my fist, but it's futile and I land on my butt in the mud with a cliched thud.

Dakota laughs, loudly, climbing off Chesney gracefully like only a girl who's been riding horses longer than she's probably walked could.

She's calming Chesney with soothing words, then turns her attention to me, still sitting in the mud pouting like a toddler.

"Need some help, Knox?" Dakota taunts, smirking cheekily as she holds out a hand to me. I consider yanking on it and pulling her down into the mud with me.

But instead, as she yanks me to my feet I inhale a deep breath, steadying myself before I snake an arm around her waist to dip her without warning.

Caz May

And I kiss her, slow to gauge her reaction. She gasps into the kiss, her hand reaching up to grip my neck, as my tongue traces her lips to deepen the kiss. And holy hell. Her kiss is innocent, but arousing beyond belief.

I want this girl, even with others in the town who are more my age trying to get with me. Dakota is kissing me as though she wants to devour me and send me to heaven and hell at the same time.

She's inexperienced and young but I'd go to hell for more of these kisses.

Panting I break our lips apart, settling her back on her feet.

She's smiling so wide I can see her white teeth.

"Wow, Knox. That was a pretty amazing first kiss."

Her first kiss. I took her first kiss. I shouldn't have done that.

"That was your first kiss, like ever?" I question, annoyed with myself for taking advantage of her.

"Yeah," she mumbles, blushing. "And it was so good."

"Well, um...I'm glad you enjoyed it," I say, inwardly cursing myself for how stupid and old I sound.

Dakota nods at me, still smiling. "I did."

I don't have anything to say, she's practically rendered me speechless with just one tantalising kiss that has me wanting more, but knowing I can't have that.

One kiss is all I can have of the beautiful Dakota, even though I already know that one kiss isn't near enough.

She takes my hand, squeezing it.

"We better be getting back. You good to get back on Chessie?"

"Not really," I admit, balling my other hand into a fist nervously. "But I probably don't have a choice."

She laughs, and it's the sweetest sound I've ever heard.

"No, unless you want to stay out here in the paddock all night."

I shake my head, laughing myself, thoughts of wild foxes attacking me filling my head.

"Yeah, I'd rather sleep in my bed, so back in the saddle it is."

She gasps at my words, licking her lips that I've just kissed, and want to kiss again with her teasing me like that, but I don't.

We climb back on Chesney, and this time, even though it hurts—because I can't have her—I hold onto her waist tightly until we're back at the barn.

It will be the last time I hold her tight, and that very thought hurts my heart a lot more than it should.

Caz May

Twenty One

Dakota

We haven't had Assembly at school in months— since Principal Reading first started at school and told us about the new school uniform—and I'm kinda nervous about it. I have no idea what this assembly is about, but the corridors are full of my classmates talking, spreading rumours.

Take My Heart

Following Ava into the hall, we take a seat, and I bounce my knees nervously whilst waiting for the assembly to start.

"You ok, Kota?" my best friend asks, a hand on my knees to calm me.

"Yeah, I just hate assembly. Always feel like it's going to be bad news."

"Yeah, assembly sucks," Ava says with a laugh, when principal Reading steps up onto the stage, stepping up to the podium. He announces loudly into the microphone, "If you could take your seats quickly, and quieten down, thank you."

The room falls silent, except for the squeak of the fold down seats. It's really quiet, and that makes me even more nervous about why we're having assembly.

Mr Reading clears his throat and starts to speak slowly, "Students, as you may have heard in the news, a member of our student body is currently in custody for murder charges." My heart stops, and then races. He just said 'murder', so casually as though that's not one of the most heinous words ever.

He lets the words sink in, after the collective shocked gasp and chattering settles down. Hands shoot up to ask questions. He points at a student who stands up to ask, "Can you tell us who, Mr Reading?"

"Yes, it is Braeden Chappell. I do not know any more details, other than that the deceased is reported to be his older brother. I will not tolerate rumours and chatter about the matter from here on out."

"Thanks, Mr Reading," the student replies sitting down. Mr Reading nods, before dismissing the student body.

I'm feeling really spooked, shocked that Braeden could do something like that. I don't really know him, other than the fact he's the soccer team captain.

As we head to our lockers, I say to Ava, "I didn't know he had a brother."

My best friend nods at me, opening her locker.

"Yeah, I feel like we don't know him at all," she begins, adding with a bit more confidence in her tone, "But I don't think he's a murderer."

"Yeah, I don't know," I reply, opening my own locker to grab my books out.

Ava is glaring at me, and I have no idea what she's feeling. She's always been more friendly with Braeden, with all the boys in our year level.

x"He has like tattoos and stuff," I blurt out. "He kinda scares me."

Ava laughs at my innocent admission.

"Just because he has tattoos doesn't mean he's a bad scary guy, Kota," she says, adding with a smile, "Zeke has tattoos."

I nod, because it's true that her boyfriend has tattoos, but I know him.

"Yeah, but Zeke is like a teddy bear," I tell her, laughing myself when I add, "And he's...like nice."

Ava smiles wide, blushing when she says, "Yeah, he's my Zekey bear."

I don't know what else to say, and we start heading to class. Ava breaks the silence between us we walk, "Trust me, Kota. Braeden is a nice guy. Misunderstood, but nice."

I nod, then shake my head when I reply cautiously, "Whatever you say, A. He still scares me a little."

She laughs, opening the door to her history class, as I continue down the corridor to my english class.

I'm thinking about Braeden, and wondering if he really did murder his brother. It makes me wonder if you really know the people around you, the people you see everyday.

My mind wanders to Dr Ellersan—Knox—and the kiss we shared the other day. It made me want to get to know him more, but I'm scared about that too.

I need to put on my big girl knickers, and grow up.

Knox might really want me then, and even though I'm scared I want him to want me.

Caz May

Twenty One

Dakota

A few weeks later

After school, I'd met Braeden at the front gate. We hadn't exchanged a word, as he followed me onto the bus and sitting next to me I can't bring myself to look at him, opting instead to stare out the window.

I scoot so far across the seat so I don't have to touch him—even a little bit—because I feel betrayed. I don't

Take My Heart

want to believe what he'd told me at lunchtime—that he's my half brother—because that not so little tidbit of information makes my whole home life a lie. It means I've been lied to by the people I love the most, the people who supposedly are my family.

I'm also staring out the window, because I'm too shy to say anything to Braeden. I don't usually talk to guys—with the exception of Knox lately—but he's different, and I'm still nervous around Braeden even though he'd been acquitted of all charges in relation to his brothers' death.

"Dakota, are you ok?" Braeden suddenly asks, touching my thigh and immediately taking it back, when I look at him in horror. I'm sure the gesture was supposed to be comforting but I'm jumpy and edgy from the news he'd told me.

"Yes, but I'm not talking to you," I snap angrily at him, defensive.

"Um, ok," he stammers, sounding as though my abruptness hurts.

"Did I do something wrong?" he asks.

I glance at him then, sniffing back my tears. My eyes feel puffy, and inflamed from not letting the tears out.

"You know what you said, Braeden. Just leave me alone until we get to my house."

He doesn't reply, just waiting until the bus stops and I get up from my seat, shoving him in the back as he stands as well. I'm being mean to him, I know that but I don't have anything to say.

Caz May

We disembark the bus, and I kick the dirt as we head to the farm gate.

As always the gate screeches as I open it and he follows me down the driveway towards the farmhouse. He's a damn slowpoke, taking tentative steps as though he's afraid of animals running out to attack him.

Once at the house, I drop my schoolbag at the door and kick off my shoes into the pile at the door. Braeden kicks off his shoes as well, gulping when I open the front door, and call out, "Mum, I'm home."

Braeden follows me inside into our huge kitchen. Mum has set the dining table for six people with cutlery and plates and when Braeden and I walk in—my blonde, petite mum—turns to face us.

Rushing into the room I hug her and her eyes catch Braeden's behind me. I can feel her looking at him and it stirs up a weird feeling in my guts.

"Oh, and you've bought a boy home," Mum states, breaking the hug when I nod at her.

"Yes, this is Braeden..." I start but I get cut off by mum.

"Braeden Chappell," mum finishes for me.

Braeden nods, and I gape in shock that mum knows his name. Braeden doesn't even get to say a word, to greet mum or anything before she crosses the room, hugging him and bursting into tears.

When mum breaks the hug she says apologetically to Braeden, "I'm so sorry Braeden. So sorry for everything."

Take My Heart

"It's ok. I um...actually don't know much," Braeden admits, his head down.

"Sit down," Mum says, looking at me and adding, "sweetie, could you add another place to the table?"

Braeden sits down at the end of the table and mum sits next to me, sighing and brushing off her hands on her apron.

"Ok, so tell me what you know about your family? My family?" Mum says to him calmly.

"Well, not much," Braeden admits, grabbing out what I'm presuming is the copy of the birth certificate from his pocket to show her. Putting it on the table he continues speaking, "Basically, my dad and my little brother were killed by Lilith when I was six."

Mum nods, telling him to continue. "And I'd been living with my older brother Carson since then. We got into a fight a couple weeks ago, and he shot himself."

"Oh my, Braeden. I'm sorry to hear that," Mum coos, even though she's shocked by that news. I'm not sure how I'm feeling. I honestly had no idea about Braeden's home life. It seems really horrible.

"Don't be," Braeden says, not fazed. "Carson wasn't a good brother. He was involved in all manner of crimes, and he abused me physically for years."

"We should've done something. Honestly I had no idea about Carson."

"Yeah, it's ok, Mrs Neelson. You didn't know."

Mum gives him a smile, telling him, "Call me Matilda, and honestly I should've done more for Dillon's son."

Braeden gulps and sniffs back tears at the mention of his father's name. Admittedly that tugs at my heart.

"So, can you tell me what happened? He asks mum, a hopeful hitch in his voice.

"Of course," mum says, sincerely. "We knew this day would come eventually. Dakota, sit down please. You need to hear this too."

I sit on the opposite side of the table, putting my elbows on the edge, watching as mum unfolds the birth certificate, and glances over it quickly.

"Ok, so I'll start by letting you know that your father loved you both," she tells us, glancing at me for a moment before she continues, "but because of the fact that both Lilith and I got pregnant only months apart, we decided to keep it from you and raise you separately. I loved Dillon, but Martin didn't want any controversy so we kept it quiet."

I'm flabbergasted, utterly speechless. I can't bring myself to look at Braeden, even when I start to sob, and have to sniff back the tears.

"It broke my heart to not see you after you were born, Braeden. I really wanted to be a part of your life too, but Dillon wouldn't have it," Mum says, really sincerely. "And he pushed me away, not even wanting to see Dakota either.

Take My Heart

"He said it hurt too much to look at her, because she looked so much like me. And we couldn't be together."

"So, do you know what happened with Lilith after?" Braeden asks, cringing when he says his mum's name, as though speaking the she devils name will summon her, or something worse.

"Not much. You probably know more than I do about those six years before Dillon's death."

He nods, asking, "Yeah, did you come to his funeral?"

"Yes, but only the church service. It was quite confronting. And I feel horrible that I didn't support you more."

"I appreciate you telling me now," Braeden admits.

I need to say something now I've absorbed the words mum has just admitted.

"So, dad isn't my dad?" I ask confusedly.

Mum looks across at me, her expression flat.

"No dear, not by blood, but in every other way."

"Great," I snap, frustrated and angry, so much so that I swear, "Just fucking great."

I never swear and mum chastises me for it, "Language Dakota Abigail. Be thankful you were raised in a loving family."

"Whatever, mum," I snap.

"Mind yourself, young lady. I will not stand for this behaviour in this house, with company who will be a part of your life."

Mum stands then, heading over to the oven that is beeping because dinner is ready.

Pulling out the roast beef—that smells delicious—she turns to ask Braeden, "Braeden, dear, will you be staying for dinner?"

"I'd love that," he replies with a smile. "Can I help with anything?"

"No thanks, dear, go with Dakota to wash up and dinner will be served when Martin comes in."

Huffing as I stand up, I nod at Braeden and then stomp down the hallway. He follows me, taking in each room with open doors. He watches my younger siblings who are playing in one bedroom, and I smile at them as we head down the hallway to the bathroom.

Quickly we wash our hands, glancing at each other. I'm giving him dagger eyes. I don't really need another brother, or another sibling in general. They're pains in my butt, and Braeden still kinda scares me, even though now he doesn't seem as scary.

"Dakota, do we still have a problem? Your mum has confirmed you're my sister. I'd honestly like to get to know you and your family more."

"I don't need another brother," I hurl at him, shoving past him to head to my bedroom.

After following me, he stops in the open doorway, hesitant to enter my space. I don't want him here in my house, my room.

I shouldn't be making him feel not welcome though, because that's not me. I've always been told I'm sweet— and a little bit sassy—but kindhearted and nice to everyone. But I'm scared and wary of Braeden, nervous around him still, because he's a boy my age.

Sitting cross legged on my bed I'm staring down at my fingers, whilst Braeden still stands in my doorway. He breaks the tension and silence with my name as a question, "Dakota?"

I huff, gazing up at him.

"What Braeden? Why don't you just fuck off, like you basically told me to."

I'm irate, and I shouldn't be, but he's upset me.

"Well, um...I..." he stammers and I cock my head to the side, again huffing in annoyance.

"Why are you so upset with me about this?" he asks.

"Because you blamed me for your dad and brother's death," I bellow at him standing up and stalking towards him.

"Oh right, I did, and I'm sorry for saying that," he tells me, his tone sincere and apologetic.

"You should be," I sass with my hand on my hip.

"I was just upset, and looking for someone to blame other than Lilith. I didn't know the truth," Braeden admits, again seeming sincere, and cringing when he said, 'Lilith'.

"And now that you do?" I enquire, raising an eyebrow at him.

Caz May

He laughs, smiling at me and saying, "I take it back. Lilith is the only one to blame for those actions. I just want to get to know you, my sister."

He elbows me in the side, playfully, still with the smile.

"Fine, I'll get to know you, but only because you're my brother," I jeer giving him a cheeky smile back.

We both laugh then, and he pulls me into a hug that I can't refuse. And don't want to refuse.

"Thanks, Dakota. I've always wanted a family who cares about me."

I laughs again and smile. "Yeah, no shortage of love in this house. Let's head back to the kitchen. Sounds like dad is home."

He follows me back out into the kitchen, where the rest of my family—our family—is seated at the dining table. He takes a seat next to me, and we tuck into mum's famous Roast beef, with vegetables and gravy. The look on Braeden's face as he eats is utter love. And it makes me happy for some reason.

As we eat, everyone chats, and I promise myself that I'll give Braeden a chance. A promise to myself that I'll get to know my brother.

Twenty Three

Knox

*I*t's been a month—and even with being super busy in the clinic—I still can't stop thinking about Dakota. And the kiss we shared on the farm. It was brazen of me to kiss her like that, so passionately and out of the blue. It was brazen to kiss her in general.

When I shouldn't be thinking about her she's on my mind, constantly distracting me from what I need to be

Caz May

doing. When another blonde client was in today, I got distracted with my thoughts—picturing her as Dakota—and nearly poked the poor dog with his injection up the butt, instead of in the crook of his neck.

I'm angry with myself—with the beautiful Dakota—for being a constant distraction. A distraction that's causing me to falter in my work, and causing me to be sporting a semi all day.

I'm so turned on by the end of the day—with her constantly on my mind—that getting into the shower my hand grips my dick, stroking it to full attention.

As I jerk off—with the warm water cascading down over me—I close my eyes and think about her, about kissing her and her innocent response.

Of wanting more, all of her. To have her completely, and strip her of every piece of her clothing, before I take her innocence.

I shouldn't be thinking these thoughts, shouldn't be jerking off so hard I'm shooting my load against the tiles with a bellowing groan. I'm thinking about—and just came —thinking about fucking a seventeen year old. Surely that makes me some kind of sick, perverted arsehole.

Turning off the shower, I get out, panicking as I can hear pounding on the vet clinic door.

Quickly I wrap a towel around my waist, crossing my fingers it's my imagination as I go to investigate.

Take My Heart

At the door I find Dakota standing outside in a ball gown, smiling at me. She has Benji on a leash sitting next to her on the edge of the long beige ball gown.

I can see her feet peeking out, with white—but dirty—converse sneakers on.

Opening the door, and leaning against it with a hand on the edge of the towel so it doesn't fall down I gulp.

"Dakota, um...what are you doing here? And in a ball gown?" I question her, stupidly.

"It's the year twelve ball tonight," she tells me, still with the mega smile when she continues before I can say a word, "But I didn't have anyone to go with, and I wanted to see you." She's rushing out the words, as though she's embarrassed and the blush that colours her cheeks as she eyes me confirms that or is quite possibly telling me she's turned on; like I am.

"I like what I'm seeing," she says, giggling.

Mentally telling my dick to calm down I shake my head.

"Dakota please, you need to go home," I plead, taking a little bit of a step back before adding, "I can't go to the ball with you."

She pouts at me, and fuck me...I want to kiss her again. And do so much more with my innocent girl.

"We don't have to go to the ball," she says nonchalantly, as if it's a question. "We could have our own ball here."

Caz May

Oh yes we could...but we can't and I need to shut her down. I need to stop her advances—her sweet innocent seduction—before I go to far.

"I'm sorry if you thought something was happening with us, but that kiss was a mistake, Dakota," I tell her, feeling my heart constricting. "It can't happen again."

She starts to sob then, which turns into blubbering crying when she pleads, "It wasn't a mistake."

"You're seventeen,Dakota," I remind her. "We can't be together."

I want to add even though I want us to be, but I don't. I kissed her—and I shouldn't have done—so I can't get her hopes up by leading her on like some horny teenage boy.

"Fine!" she snaps. "I just thought you were different to guys my age, but you're not!"

Her words are angry, and bending down to pick up Benji, I'm given a view of her cleavage that makes me groan, because just that hint of skin has me hard again. She huffs and leaves, stomping her converses on the footpath as she trudges away. I almost call out to her—curse it all, I want her—but I stop myself, heading to my bedroom frustrated and turned on again.

I need a damn root, from someone my own age, or I'm going to go down a bad road, straight to hell.

Twenty Four

Dakota

Rushing away from the clinic I text Ava.

A you home yet?

Nearly, Kota. Are you ok?

Nope. I'm coming over. With Benji.

Ok meet you at mine.

Caz May

Getting to my best friend's house I knock hard on the door, holding Benji under my arm, against my hip.

Considering I ran here, I'm surprised Ava beat me and she's opening the door to me. She's still wearing her tight electric green body con dress, and gapes when she takes in my outfit.

"Hey Kota," she greets me, ushering me inside."Why are you in a ball gown?" She questions, closing the door once I step across the threshold.

I gulp, holding in my stupid laugh.

"Long story, can we talk in your room?"

"Of course," Ava replies, already about to go upstairs to her room.

Once in her bedroom we plonk down on the beanbags by her bed and Ava grabs Benji for a hug, muttering something about how cute my puppy is, whilst I stay silent.

A couple minutes later, after she's finished hugging my puppy, she asks eagerly, "So what's up bestie?"

I sigh, taking in a deep breath that I exhale as I reply, "So much, A. I don't know where to start."

Ava laughs, teasing me, "Maybe with why you're in a ball gown?"

"Um...yeah...I think I should tell you something else first," I reply, blushing with guilt. "I've been a bad friend, A," I admit, expecting her to agree with me, but instead she questions me, "Why do you say that?"

"Because I've been lying to you, and hiding things from you," I confess, hanging my head down so I don't have to look her in the eye.

Glancing up tentatively she looks upset but kinda excited at my crazy admission.

"Like what? Tell me, Kota," she pleads, giving me her best puppy dog eyes, just like Benji who has me wrapped around his tiny paw.

"Well, I found out something about Braeden, and he's not so scary now."

"Ooo what?" Ava shrieks excitedly.

"He's my brother, like my actual blood related half brother. We have, or had the same dad."

"Wow!" Ava calls out, "Is that all?"

"No, I also kissed Knox, Dr Ellersan. I made him come out to the farm, and we went for a ride and he kissed me, and it was so amazing."

"Oh shit Kota, that's so cool about Brae. And wow, your first kiss!"

"Yeah the Braeden thing is crazy and cool. He still scares me a little, but I don't know it's weird that I feel like there is a connection between us. I want to get to know him more now."

"For sure. And you should. He needs family now, after everything."

"Yeah," I mumble, not sure what else to say after letting out my secrets.

"So kissing Dr Ellersan? An older man, huh?" Ava teases.

I giggle, blushing with my eager reply, "Honestly It was so amazing, A. But I went to see him tonight and he shoved me out the door, telling me it was a mistake."

"Oh that's shit. Maybe he doesn't want to take advantage of you, or he has a girlfriend his age or something?" She surmises?, giving me a slight smile.

"I don't think he does, but I don't know, A. I really like him, like a lot."

"I know, Kota. But he's older," she says softly, then adds louder, "You should try to find a guy our age."

I scoff, shaking my head because she knows how I feel about guys—idiotic boys—our age.

"I don't want another guy. Especially one our age. They're all idiots who only think with their dicks." I blush, thinking about the outline of Knox's dick in the towel. I think he was turned on, because I saw the exact same outline in his jeans when we kissed.

"Why're you blushing, Kota?" Ava taunts with a smirk.

"Because I saw his dick tonight."

"What?! Are you serious?"

"Well, sorta," I admit, blushing even more, because I'm talking about sexy things with my best friend. "He was only wearing a towel and he was like you know...hard when I was talking to him."

Take My Heart

"Oh wow, Kota," Ava says with a laugh. "I think he likes you too, but he just doesn't want to get involved because you're not eighteen."

"So what?" I protest, huffing. "I'm not innocent. I'm a virgin, but I know stuff, and I've seen dirty stuff."

"Sure, Kota," Ava again replies with a cheeky laugh that makes me want to poke her. "Just give it some time. Maybe he'll change his mind."

"I hope so, cause I think I could fall in love with him, A."

I think I already am in love with him, but I'm not going to admit that out loud. And thats why his rejection is hurting so much. It's the only thing that makes sense.

"I know Kota, I know."

"Can I stay tonight?" I ask, adding a follow up, "It's too late to go home."

"Of course, bestie," Ava says, groaning as she struggles to get out of the beanbag. "I'll grab a blanket for Benji to sleep on and you can grab some pjs out of my drawers."

She leaves the room to get Benji a blanket and I stand awkwardly from the beanbag. I grab out some pjs, laughing at Benji who is doing zoomies around Ava's room.

Getting out of my dress I start thinking about whether Knox really did want me to leave. His body was saying he wanted me to stay but his words said no, and I laugh thinking of Ava calling him Dr Ellersan in a cheeky tone, because that makes me wonder what it would be like to play doctors and nurses with him. And that is not like me. It's dirty, naughty thoughts that make me feel all tingly.

I'm in love with Dr Knox Ellersan and somehow I'm going to make him fall in love with me too, even if I have to be naked so he loves my body first.

Take My Heart

Twenty Five

Knox

*C*lutching the paper tray with two coffees—one for me, one for Andrea—I'm heading back to the clinic in a hurry, when in my haste I bump into two people and a dog.

Glancing up I'm staring at Dakota. She has a boy her age with her, and is tightly holding Benji's leash.

Caz May

Her outfit is cute—sexy—consisting of tight dark jeans, a brown, short leather jacket with a white tight t-shirt underneath, teamed with beige ugg boots. She's staring back at me, her eyes darkening as she looks at my chest, as though she's imagining me naked. It's awkward.

I'm tongue tied—like a teenage boy—because quite frankly Dakota takes my breath away. She's sassy, and a stunner, and has no idea.

Panicking because I'm standing in the middle of the street, thinking about stripping Dakota naked, I stumble as I try to rush away, and subsequently spill the coffee down my shirt. It's hot, burning my skin and without thinking I pull it off.

The boy standing next to Dakota is giving me an odd look, and glancing at Dakota who's eyes are nearly falling out of her head.

Stupid me for taking off my shirt.

I need to rescue this situation, get her mind out of the gutter where I put it by ripping my coffee stained t-shirt off like an idiot.

Finding my voice, I say, "Oh, Dakota, hi, I'm sorry." It's all a jumble of words, and she's just staring at my lips.

Without her reply, dropping my gaze to the ground, I ask,"How's the little Benji man doing?"

Dakota smiles wide. "He's better. Keeping him inside now. And um...yep."

Benji starts licking the coffee off the ground, and Dakota shrieks, "Oh no...um!"

Take My Heart

She scoops him up, looking worried and I chuckle.

"He'll be fine Dakota. But bring him back in straight away if he has any odd symptoms."

"I um will...thank you Dr Ellersan," she stammers, licking her lips almost suggestively. That makes my traitorous body threaten to say hello in my jeans.

"Anytime," I assure her with a nod. "Is this your boyfriend? I ask, hoping that she says no, even though that's momentarily bad.

Her and the boy laugh and Dakota says, "Oh no...this is Braeden. He's my brother."

"Oh right...well nice to meet you Braeden," I say, shaking his hand.

"Nice to meet you, Dr Ellersan," Braeden says, pulling back from the hand shake.

"I should be getting back to work," I start, stepping aside, skirting around the coffee on the ground. "You two kids have a good day."

They start to walk off, and I go back to the clinic, straight into my apartment—even though Andrea is calling out to me—and I grab another shirt.

Pulling it on I sigh in frustration, annoyed at myself that I was glad Braeden wasn't her boyfriend.

I'm falling for her, and that's wrong in so many ways.

Caz May

Twenty Six

Dakota

Putting Benji back down onto the footpath, I avert my gaze from Knox heading back to the vet clinic. It's hard not to look at his butt in his tight jeans.

Continuing walking with Braeden, he pokes me in the side, laughing hard when he asks, "You like him, huh?"

His tone is teasing, and I shrug, hoping I'm not blushing and giving myself away when I say, "Who? Huh?"

Take My Heart

"Dr Ellersan, dufus," Braeden teases, again elbowing me, and grinning as though he now knows my biggest secret. I gulp, feeling my cheeks heat.

Braeden continues with another question, "Who else would I be talking about?"

I scoff then, in an attempt to hide my real answer.

"No...he's old, Braeden."

"Whatever you say Dakota," Braeden says mocking me. "You looked at him like I look at Ar's and Bris."

Oh golly, I hope I don't look at him like that. Braeden always a dirty glint in his eyes when he looks at Ariel, and Briston too. I honestly don't get what the deal is with them. Ariel tried explaining it to me, but honestly loving two boys sounds hella complicated and really dirty and naughty.

Again I feel a blush heat my cheeks with my defensive reply, "I do not look at him...at Dr Ellersan like that."

Braeden laughs again, really chuckling when he jeers, "Yeah you do."

I want to slap my brother for being a meanie, and a dufus, but I stop myself as we've arrived at the café.

Tying Benji up outside, I give him a kiss on his fluffy head, telling him I'll only be a minute. We go inside, and line up to order our milkshakes.

Braeden keeps staring me down. And I can't escape his stare. He wants me to admit it. It being my feelings for Knox.

"Fine...nosy brother" I snigger. "I like him...and we kissed but he doesn't want me."

He again laughs. And it's so damn annoying. "You sure about that, sis?" Braeden teases. I slap his arm, and he grabs it screeching at me, "Ow, sis. That hurt!"

I laugh, mocking him, "Quit being a baby, little brother."

He humphs, shoving me in the hip as we step up to the counter to order our milkshakes. Both cookies and cream, with extra Oreo and whipped cream with chocolate sprinkles. They're truly decadent, but honestly I don't care how naughty they are when they taste so damn delicious.

It takes a couple minutes for the milkshakes to be made, and once we're back outside —milkshakes in hand, sipping on them—I untie Benji.

Braeden pauses, and pokes me in the side.

"You didn't respond before, you know if you're sure that Dr Ellersan doesn't want you."

"I'm sure Brae. He's told me as much."

He slurps his milkshake, snorting back a laugh to say in a serious tone, "He's lying Dakota. He wants you."

"Maybe. But I should move on and find a younger guy," I reply.

Braeden smiles but doesn't say anything as we continue to sip our milkshakes, heading back to the park where I parked the ute.

"Are you coming over for dinner tonight? I ask, adding, "mum's cooking a roast again."

Take My Heart

"Nah, got plans with Bris. His parents are in the city for the weekend."

"Oh right," I reply, blushing because I'm sure his plans with his 'boyfriend' are of the dirty sexual kind.

"Yes Dakota. Those kinda plans."

"Dont tease me, Brae."

"Sorry, but maybe thats whats holding Dr Ellersan back."

I shrug, annoyed at my brother for pointing out that I'm a virgin, and that an experienced man won't go for a girl, a little innocent, inexperienced girl.

But little does my brother know—and won't know, because some things are not for sharing with brothers—but I've seen some dirty things of the porn variety. And I'm going to seduce Dr Ellersan, somehow.

I want him to want me, in all kinds of dirty ways, because I want him to shred my innocence completely.

Caz May

Twenty Seven

Dakota

Scrunching my tousled beach wavy hair in my fingers, I shuffle on my feet and purse my lips telling myself to get on with it.

I came into town, driving the ute in my cowboy boots which was difficult as the thick soles made feeling the pedals extremely challenging.

And I'm standing on the footpath--outside the clinic-- wondering if the people walking past can tell I'm not

Take My Heart

wearing knickers and a bra under my tiny salmon pink shorts and white midriff-baring tank top. This outfit isn't something I'd normally wear, and going without underwear isn't either, but baring so much skin is sure to get Knox to really look at me. That's if he even comes to the door. It feels like I've been standing here for hours, softly knocking on the door.

And the panic is setting in. He's probably not even home. But I can't tell as the lights are off in the clinic, but you can't see his apartment from the front door.

I knock a bit harder, and when he comes down the hallway my heart catches in my chest, my breath stolen by how stunningly good looking he is, without even trying. He's barefoot, wearing grey trackies, and a loose white t-shirt. His hair is messy, and he runs his hand through it, yawning as he comes to unlock the door.

"Oh um, Dakota, sorry," he stammers, opening the door and roaming my barely covered body with his dark mesmerising eyes. I'm tongue-tied from staring at him, my eyes boggling with the way the veins in his arm pulse as he leans against the door.

"What're you doing here, Dakota?" he asks, huskily, stifling another yawn.

"I wanted to see you," I reply, pushing my boobs out, and jutting my hip to the side. I really have no clue how to flirt but I've watched many romance movies and those are both signature moves.

Knox sighs and even that sound from his lips sounds sexy. I've got it bad for this man.

"You can't keep coming here unannounced for no reason. People will talk. It's a small town."

His words are truth, but they aren't gospel. And I really don't actually care. People are talking about me, and my family now as it is, so what's another scandal to add to the Neelson name.

"People will talk if you keep standing there staring at me, and don't invite me inside Dr Ellersan," I taunt, feeling really brazen. There's something about Knox that makes me lose all my inhibitions.

"Fine, but nothing is going to happen." He says the words as though he's trying to convince himself.

The tension and longing for me he's feeling is radiating off his body, so he clenches his fists, his gaze dropping to my butt when I walk through the door.

Closing it behind us, he follows me down the hallway to his apartment. I can still feel his gaze on me, and I wonder if my shorts are riding up and showing my bare butt cheeks.

Getting to his apartment he bumps into me as we cross the threshold, and his hand brushes against the small of my back, heating my body instantly.

He clears his throat, his voice coming out gruffly, "This is quite the outfit, Dakota."

I turn around, stepping further back into his space. His eyes don't leave my body. And he licks his lips, again clearing his throat. I take a moment to return the lustful gaze of his body, and my pulse races into my shorts when I notice the outline of his dick in his trackies. I'd heard girls talking about guys in grey trackies before, and I'd never understood the appeal but now seeing Knox in them I totally get it.

With our eyes still roaming each other's bodies, I tease, "I wore it for you."

"You should wear more clothes around me," he says, with the same husky tone.

"And why is that, Dr Ellersan?" I taunt, loving the groan he can't help but let fall from lips.

"Please Dakota, you need to stop," he demands, stalking closer to me into the open lounge room.

"Stop what?" I goad him again, hooking my fingers into the side of my shorts.

"Everything, Dakota. Coming here, wearing ridiculously sexy outfits, just everything."

"What if I don't want to stop?" I ask, pouting at him.

"Then I won't be able to stop myself from taking advantage of you."

"I want you to," I tell him, exhaling a shaky breath when I add, "take my virginity,"

Knox groans, cursing, "fuck Dakota. You're seventeen and a fucking virgin. Do you know what you're asking of me?"

"Yes, I want you, Knox. Fuck me, please," I plead, a rasp in my voice.

Caz May

He groans, closing the final distance between us. My legs hit the back of the couch and he grips my waist, pulling me against his body.

"I'm not fucking you, Dakota," he tells me, and I huff, annoyed so much I'm pouting again, and I actually grunt.

"Yet," Knox says, before crushing his lips to mine and sending me to heaven with his dizzying kiss.

I know I have no other kisses to compare with, but kissing Knox Ellersan is amazing, and I want to kiss him for the rest of my life.

I think I'm in love with this feeling, this total package of a man.

Take My Heart

Twenty Eight

Knox

I'm kissing her.

I shouldn't be kissing her, but it's happening. And damn, this beautiful, inexperienced girl is kissing me senseless. I can't believe how much it's turning me on.

Without breaking the kiss, I slide my hands in the back of her shorts, finding she's naked underneath. Her skin is soft and her arse pert, firm, and she lets out a slight whimper which causes our kiss to end.

Caz May

"Damn," I curse, gazing over her barely clothed body, wondering what her young body looks like beneath. I now know she's not wearing knickers, and I guess from the way her nipples are pressing against the tank top that she's not wearing a bra either. It's damn brazen, and incredibly alluring.

With her eyes not leaving mine she whispers, "I'm not wearing any underwear."

"I can see that kitten," I tell her.

"Touch me, Knox," she purrs again, her voice raspy. I swear for a girl so innocent she knows exactly how to turn a man on.

kissing her again, intensely, my hands everywhere--all over her heavenly body--until they're in the back of her tiny pink shorts again and I'm pushing them down her legs. They drop to the floor, and she shivers from the cool air hitting her core.

Stopping our kiss again, I gaze at her lifting off her top, over her head, and throwing it aside I admire her perfect tits. Round, and the perfect size to take in my hand, with hard bright rosy pink nipples.

I groan, lowering my gaze towards her pussy which is all natural, a bush of pale blonde hair between her legs. She's utterly mesmerising, and not shying away from my lustful gaze on her, like I thought she would.

"Fuck Dakota," I moan, biting down on my lip whilst I scan her body again. "You're so beautiful. Pure, natural... and..." I want to say, 'mine' but it feels too presumptuous,

Take My Heart

but honestly I'm thinking it and clearly she as well, because she purrs back in response, "Yours."

I kiss her again, with the same passion as before, but this time deepening the kiss with tongue, tasting her and devouring her. My hand drops to between her legs, a finger touching her clit to find she's wet. She murmurs, practically mewling at my touch.

"Damn kitten, you're turned on," I whisper against her lips, before she's pulling back a little and her eyes darken as she locks them on me.

For a moment, I'm worried I've gone to far, but then she mewls, "Only for you, Knox. I want you to do dirty things to me."

Oh god, I'm going to hell. Dropping to my knees, I crouch down so my lips are right there, right where all I need to do is dart my tongue out, and I'd be going down on her. And I do just that, kissing her clit, and sucking on it.

"Oh," she gasps, suddenly gripping my hair as she rocks her pelvis on my face. With my tongue out, she fucks my face, riding my tongue desperately, moaning so loudly my whole apartment is filled with the sound. With my tongue deep inside her pussy, her hips still, as I kiss her pussy again, and she comes, her pelvis trembling and her legs shaking so hard she grips the edge of the couch with her hand, moaning out a loud, "Oh, wow!"

Pulling back my face is covered in her cum, and I lick my lips as I stand up.

Dakota is grinning, and I'm stupidly chuffed I've given her such a wide grin.

"That was amazing," she says, still not able to get rid of her pretty grin.

"First orgasm, huh?" I tease, with a smirk that makes her laugh.

"Yeah, and wow," she says, blushing, and asking, "Was it good for you?"

"Only you'd ask that kitten," I tease again, making her blush deepen.

"But yes, kitten, tasting you coming on my face was amazing."

"Can I try it?" she questions, shocking me so much with her words that I gasp with my reply, "Try what, kitten?"

"My come," she declares, raspy, and as though her statement is a normal thing for an innocent girl to be asking.

I gulp, asking, "Are you sure?"

"Yeah," she replies nodding.

I don't say anything, nor give her a second to think more about her request before I'm kissing her and she's licking her come off my lips, moaning.

Breaking the kiss, she licks her lips, claiming, "It's different."

I'm watching her, still licking her lips, wondering what she's thinking in the moment of silence. But I don't have

Take My Heart

to wait too long, as she asks, "Do you taste like that as well?"

I laugh, shaking my head and responding, "No kitten. But let's not get ahead of ourselves tonight."

"But I want to taste you, Dr Ellersan," she murmurs, purring my name which turns me on a lot more than it should.

I shouldn't want her to suck my dick. I really shouldn't want anything more from her, but god I want it all.

Despite my desperation, I reply, "Please Dakota don't say things like that. I'd love that, but I've already gone too far with you."

"Can I see it then, at least?" Dakota asks innocently.

"See what?" I ask, even though I know exactly what she means, I want to hear her say it.

"Your dick. I can see it's hard."

This girl is going to kill me slow.

"Yeah kitten," I say, dropping my trackies to the floor without a second thought.

Caz May

Twenty Nine

Dakota

Watching Knox intently I gasp seeing his dick when he drops his trackies to the floor. His dick is hard, and poking towards me.

Tentatively—still staring—I reach out, touching him, and he moans.

"Does that feel good?" I ask, a nervous rasp in my voice. I've just touched his dick, his hard dick, and it feels so smooth, soft, like velvet brushing my fingertips.

"Amazing," he moans, biting down on his lip.

Take My Heart

"So I'm doing it right?" I question.

"Yeah, kitten, but not here," he stammers. I like this kitten nickname. It's cute.

"Oh...um...ok," I stammer back when Knox takes my hand, leading me across the lounge room to his bedroom door.

Gently pulling me inside the room, he stops at the edge of the bed, his knees hitting it. Falling back against the sheets he brings me down with him, so I'm on top of him and he's kissing me again before I can even think.

I can feel his hard dick between us, right where he licked me before. And the kiss is incredible. The man can sure kiss. I honestly don't get why people don't kiss all day and night. It's so good.

Without warning, he shifts back, and yanks off his t-shirt, throwing it on the bed.

Looking down at him, I sigh, running my hands all over him, down the length of his chest and back to his dick which I stroke up and down in a soft grip.

"Fuck Dakota," he curses loudly, lifting his head off the bed to watch. "What're you doing to me?"

His question is confusing because what I'm doing seems obvious to me, so I reply softly, "Touching you."

"Yeah, but damn kitten," he groans, adding huskily, "no one's touch has ever felt like this."

"Really?" I question, nervously laughing.

"Yeah, kitten," he responds with a nod towards his crotch. "You're going to make me come."

Caz May

Those words make me blush, as I keep stroking his dick. It starts to throb in my hand and I'm captivated as his come spurts out of the tip, all over his stomach. Dipping my finger into the sticky mess on his skin, I put the finger to my lips and taste him. The taste makes me grimace, and he laughs at my shocked expression.

"Taste salty, huh, kitten?" he asks me.

"Yeah," I reply with a laugh.

Gripping my neck he pulls me down for a kiss, that sends a shockwave to my lower body, a pulse like a heartbeat between my legs.

I don't know how to process that, what that feeling means that I only get when Knox is touching or kissing me. I've watched dirty things on my laptop in bed at night, and although they intrigue me, they don't make me feel like that.

Knox moves to get off the bed, making me stand up as he heads to the ensuite.

In the doorjamb, looking all tempting, he says huskily, "Come shower with me, kitten." It's not a request, but a demand. And I'm loving him wanting me. Tonight has been incredible.

Going into the ensuite, a nervous flutter of butterflies hit my stomach as I get into the shower with him.

We don't exchange words as he washes me, lathering soap over my belly, and between my legs with his hard body pressed against my butt. His gentle touch is making me feel so loved. He hasn't said anything remotely like the word love to me, but his actions are loving and caring.

Turning in his arms, I grab the soap and wash him as well, dropping it on the tiled floor when I stretch up to kiss him.

"Thank you for tonight, Knox," I say, kissing him again before whispering against his lips, "I'm falling for you."

He doesn't voice a reply, just kisses my forehead before turning the water off, and getting out of the shower. He wraps a fluffy towel around my shoulders, drying my skin and warming me up.

I've honestly just lied to him because I'm not falling for him.

I'm in love with him.

I'm in love with Dr Knox Ellersan. But I know it's not a good idea to voice that to him.

He may have given in to being with me—despite telling me I'm seventeen and he can't—but he's cautious, and it's not the time to voice my real feelings. I'm innocent, but not stupid.

After we've dried off, dropping the towels on the ensuite floor he takes my hand, leading me back to his bed. Pulling back the sheets we slide under the covers together. He doesn't say anything, just kisses me, passionately. I'm never going to get enough of being with him, and I'm enjoying every kiss and touch, hoping that it won't be the last.

Caz May

Breaking the kiss, he gazes into my eyes, softly murmuring, "Goodnight, kitten."

I give him a soft kiss, squirming closer to him and closing my eyes as we fall asleep in each other's arms.

Thirty

Knox

*W*aking up beside a sleeping Dakota, my dick is hard, but she looks so peaceful I don't want to wake her.

I roll out of bed carefully prying her grip off of me, quickly taking care of my hard on in the bathroom before heading into the kitchen.

My head is still in a spin about last night, from kissing her, touching her and tasting her. It was wrong on so many

Caz May

levels, but I haven't felt this good in months, years, if ever being honest. There's something about her, the innocent sexy minx she is. How she's alluring without even meaning to be.

Like right now, as she comes into the kitchen stretching her arms above her head with only my t-shirt on. She's absolutely beguiling.

I busy myself with getting out the ingredients to make pancakes, turning away from her sauntering into the kitchen. If I don't I'll be taking her back to bed for a repeat of last night, and even more wicked delights. My dick is aching in my boxers just thinking about having all of my kitten.

Starting on the pancakes, I'm shocked when she steps up behind me, wrapping her arms around my waist.

"Good morning, Dr Ellersan." God, it kills me when she calls me that. It's naughty and teases me, the way she purrs it all raspy.

Cracking the egg into the bowl, I groan and turn around to kiss her. I'd much rather have her for breakfast, but I need to tamp down my desire for her.

"Good morning, kitten. You good with pancakes for breakfast?"

"Yes thanks, I love pancakes."

"Great, take a seat, they'll be ready soon."

She follows my direction, taking a seat on a stool at the breakfast bar. I can feel her eyes on me—on my butt specifically—as my back is turned whilst I'm preparing the

Take My Heart

pancakes. It's extremely unnerving, but also exciting. Dakota effects me in a way no woman ever has. Just knowing she's looking at me like that has my dick stirring in my boxers. I'm a grown man, and can tell my body to not sport wood usually, but around Dakota that is tough. I honestly have no idea why the girl gets to me so much. Maybe her sweet disposition and her genuine love of animals. And also how stunningly beautiful she is.

Leaning against the bench I slide a plate of pancakes to Dakota, and laugh as she bites into them moaning as though they're the most delicious thing she's ever eaten.

Through her mouthful of food, she mumbles, "Mmm, Knox, these are so good."

"No worries, kitten. Eat up. I'm going to get dressed."

She nods, spooning another mouthful in, as I retreat to my bedroom to dress and calm my body down.

Leading Dakota out of the apartment after breakfast, I'm a bit late into the clinic. And Andrea has come in, already sitting at the reception desk firing up the computer to check the bookings for the day.

I stop at the door, my hand still entwined with Dakota's when i lean in to give her a kiss goodbye.

"I'll see you back here at six," I tell Dakota softly, as she walks out smiling at me. She nods, and I turn my attention to Andrea who is trying not to laugh.

I glare at her, but that doesn't stop her teasing, "Ooo, something happened with you and Dakota, huh?"

Caz May

"Shush you...but yes," I reply my gut twisting with the words I'm admitting. I'm wondering if telling Andrea is a bad idea. She's been a great employee so far, but we're not close friends. But she's the closest I've got to a friend so far in Lockgrove Bay.

"You sleep with her?" She asks, raising her eyebrow at me whilst she smirks.

"No," I snap, adding more calmly, "and my lips are sealed on what did happen nosy parker."

"Ok, no judgement here," she says with a friendly tone.

I feel like I've crossed a line I shouldn't have. and tonight taking Dakota out on a date is crossing another one.

"She's seventeen, and I shouldn't have done anything," I declare, shaking my head and chastising myself for the thoughts of last night crashing into my mind again.

"But you wouldn't take it back?" Andrea enquires, again suggestively quirking her eyebrow upwards.

I shake my head, not able to look at Andrea. "No...I wouldn't but I need to take things slow."

"Sounds like you're falling for her," Andrea suggests. My stomach flips with those words and I don't reply, instead I lean over the counter to look at the schedule for the day, glad it's not too stressful.

All day my date tonight with Dakota is on my mind, and I'm thankful for a fairly quiet day so I can finish up

Take My Heart

early and go to the small grocery store to grab some picnic supplies.

Still, despite the early finish at the clinic I'm in a panic putting the supplies into the basket I'd found in my kitchen, as it's nearly six and Dakota will be arriving any minute.

The apartment honestly has everything a man and his dog could need, and then some. It still surprises me, and makes me wonder about the old Vet, and why he didn't still live here and get someone else to run the clinic. Not that I mind, as I'm loving living in the space, and discovering more about Lockgrove Bay.

Putting some drinks in the basket, I smile when I hear Dakota's voice calling out, "Hello, Knox, I'm here."

"Come in, kitten. Doors open," I call back, bracing myself to see her sauntering into my space.

And man. She walks in wearing a pretty dress, with short sleeves and it barely covers her thighs. She's got her converse sneakers on again. And her hair is up in a bun, angling her beautiful features to make her appear more stunning.

Stepping into the kitchen, she stretches up on her tiptoes to kiss me, and it sets my body alight. This girl will be the death of me.

"Hello to you, Dakota."

"Hi, Knox. Where are we going on this date?"

"What's it look like, kitten?"

"A picnic date."

"Yeah, sound good to you?"

"Yes, perfect first date," she replies, giddily.

I pick up the basket, hooking it on my arm, and taking Dakota's hand in my other hand. Intertwining our fingers I lift her hand to my lips, kissing the back of it. Her eyes light up, as she smiles.

"Have you ever been on a date, kitten?"

"No, and I'm so glad my first date is with you, Dr Ellersan."

"I hope it's special enough for you," I respond, trying not to sound completely shellshocked about her never being on a date before. She's innocent, but a beautiful girl and I would've thought she'd have been on a date.

"It will be great," she tells me, still with that giddy smile on her face as I lead her out of the back door of the apartment into the backyard.

She eyes me quizzically, bending down to pat Toby as he comes bounding towards us.

"Hey, Toby," she says to my dog, patting his soft ears a bit longer before she stands up. "Are you coming with us, boy?"

Dakota looks at me for the answer Toby isn't giving her.

"Yeah, he is."

"Where are we going then, Dr Ellersan?"

I give her a smile.

"Would you believe me if I said I have my own private beach?"

Again her eyes light up with her beautiful smile.

Take My Heart

"Really? Where?"

"Just down through the trees," I reply, pointing in front of us when Dakota starts skipping ahead.

She's so carefree, and young in some ways, but I'm honestly thinking that's what is drawing me to her. I'm not old, but Dakota makes me feel young again, taking me back to my carefree teenage life when my father wasn't on my back about working for him, or being disappointed with me for my choices.

"Hurry up then, Knox," Dakota calls out, walking backwards, her dress swishing from side to side, giving me a glimpse of her flower print cotton knickers that really shouldn't be sexy but on her they are.

"I'm coming, kitten. Slow down for the old man."

I chuckle, smirking at her. And she returns the smirk, laughing when she replies, "You're not old, Knox!"

"Do you even know how old I am, Dakota?"

"Nope, don't care," she sing songs, rushing back to me and grabbing my hand. She drags me down the grass, until we're at the trees and can hear the crash of the waves on the beach.

"Wow," Dakota exclaims, taking in the private beach. "I had no idea this was here."

"Yeah, pretty special."

"It must be the other side of the bay," she informs me, glancing around before sitting down on the sand.

Putting the basket down beside her, I groan as I take a seat on the sand as well, stretching out my tired legs in front of me.

Toby is running around the beach, chasing his tail in the shallows and Dakota is watching him laughing. Her laugh is beautiful.

And watching her laughing is stirring up that lust in my belly. I need to get ahold of myself, tamp down my lust before I'm taking her virginity on the beach carelessly. She deserves more than that, more than a horny 'old' man taking advantage of her.

Putting a hand on her bare thigh, her skin instantly heats with my touch and she gasps, her laughing ceasing as her gaze turns to mine.

"Are you hungry, kitten?" I ask.

She nods, then smirks with her reply, "For you, yes."

"I meant for food, Dakota," I reply back, even though my whole body is aching for her. I want to devour her, but we need to eat.

"Fine, food, then kissing like yesterday," she huffs blushing and leaning over to peer in the picnic basket when I flip the lid open.

She licks her lips as I take out the shredded roast chicken and tomato pasta salad, before the bread rolls coated in fresh butter.

Watching her tongue tracing her lips causes my dick to jolt in my jeans, and I desperately want to kiss her. I'm such a damn pervert.

Take My Heart

Gruffly clearing my throat I grunt, "I hope this is ok."

"It's great. I love that salad. It's my favourite."

"Good to know," I reply, biting into my roll to distract myself from the seductress sitting across from me.

We eat in silence, smiling at each other between mouthfuls of food, and sips of Fanta. And once the food is finished, I hand Dakota a serviette. She dabs at the corners of her mouth, and says, "Is there dessert?"

"I've got chocolate," I say, fishing it out of the basket, and unwrapping the small piece of dark chocolate from the foil.

"Mmm, yummy," Dakota murmurs, taking a bite as I hold it up to her lips. After swallowing she licks her lips, watching me watch her.

"Aren't you having any?"

I shake my head.

"I'd love something else for dessert, kitten," I tease, dropping the chocolate back into the basket and shoving it aside.

Grabbing her around the waist, inching closer I push her back down on the sand gently, before taking her mouth with mine in a kiss. She moans against my mouth, wrapping her hands around my neck to pull me closer, as the kiss deepens and I can taste the chocolate she's just consumed on her tongue that laces with mine.

As we kiss, devouring each other I slide my hand up her thigh to her girly knickers, brushing a finger over the

Caz May

fabric, at her clit. Her knickers are damp, and with my touch, she moans, breaking the kiss.

Her lustful gaze is on mine, our foreheads touching.

And she murmurs softly, "I...I...think I'm in love with you, Knox."

My heart skips. And pulling back a little so I can see her face, and the flush of her cheeks at her admission I caress her cheek when I admit, "I'm feeling something for you, Dakota, but we need to take it slow until you're eighteen."

"I know," she agrees, and I kiss her again.

I'm not going to admit it to her, but fuck me dead, I'm falling for the girl and I don't want our night to finish here on the beach.

The sun is beginning to set, bringing mosquitos with it, so breaking the kiss, I sit up smiling at her.

"We should probably head back to the house before we get eaten by mosquitoes."

"Yeah, those devils love me for some reason."

I help her stand up, and we brush the sand off our butts before I pick up the basket and take her hand to head back up to the house. I whistle for Toby to follow and we run together, racing inside the house where Dakota shoves me down on the couch, kissing me again before I can even think. She will be the death of me.

Dakota

Back at his, barely a minute after we get inside I push him down on the couch without any resistance from him. And I kiss him, getting lost in him.

My hands have a mind of their own, slipping under his t-shirt to touch his abs that I love are scattered with soft blonde hairs. He shivers at my touch, as my hands edge closer to the waistband of his jeans.

Moaning he breaks the kiss, sitting up a little to pull off his t-shirt. He's smirking at me, and I gasp.

"You're sexy, Dr Ellersan," I trill, flicking the button of his jeans open, and sliding the zipper down to touch his dick through his jocks. He's not hard but my touch makes his dick throb.

He kisses me, glaring at me with darkened eyes.

"Take this dress off, kitten."

Smiling, I grab the hem of my dress pulling it off and throwing it on the floor.

I'm not wearing a bra, and Knox gasps, yanking me down to kiss my boob, biting my nipple. It stings but feels so good, sending that tingly feeling into my knickers.

Pulling back, I shift in his lap, grabbing the waistband of his jeans.

"I want these off, Dr Ellersan."

He smiles at me, wickedly with a quirk of his eyebrows.

"Only if you take off those super cute knickers, kitten."

I stand from the couch, and watching each other we slowly take off our remaining clothes, dropping them into a pile on the floor.

Again I'm naked in front of him, and my stomach flops with the way he looks at me like I'm the most beautiful girl he's ever seen.

Grabbing me around the waist he pulls me back into his lap, and we fall back onto the couch again.

My crotch is right at his. And looking down at him, I sigh, losing any inhibitions I have, any worry in my mind as I start to rub on his dick, back and forth down his growing length. It feels so good, it causes a pulsing between my legs. I'm all wet down there and I'm coating his dick in that wetness as I keep rubbing on it.

His dick gets even harder under me, and the tip nearly goes inside me.

I really, really want it to.

That would mean we would be having sex, I think.

Without warning he grabs my hips, stilling me, and he comes, the hot, white stickiness spurting out of the tip and over his belly. He makes all sorts of sexy groaning noises when he does that.

"Damn, kitten, that was hot," he tells me, pulling me down by the hips for a dirty kiss.

Against my lips, he whispers huskily, "I want you to do something really dirty for me."

"What's that?" I question, biting down on my lip. I'm hoping he says that he wants to have sex with me because

I'm still feeling really tingly and excited from rubbing on his dick. And I really want to go all the way with him.

I'm looking down at him, and he caresses my cheek with the back of his hand.

"I want you to fuck my face kitten."

I gasp because that sounds dirty and awkward.

"How do I do that?" I question.

Knox laughs, making his chest vibrate under my palms that are resting against his abs.

"You will sit on my face, Dakota," he tells me, all stern and demanding, before adding in a strained husky voice, "so bring that dripping cunt up here."

My mouth falls open, hearing that really dirty word from his lips. It makes me tingle even more, causes a heartbeat to thrum through my whole body.

I move up towards his face, and he grips my hips, lining up my centre with his mouth. And then without any warning, his tongue starts licking me there, like he did the other night, but at this angle, it feels different.

I can't help but rock my pelvis up and down on his tongue as he licks me. It feels so good, all wet and oh my golly I can't even describe it. I want to scream, but in a good way. Knox is moaning, licking me and kissing me there, and I buck my hips harder against his face, feeling as though I'm about to explode.

I'm riding his face like I'm in the saddle, and a silly thought comes to mind about the time when I was thirteen and I was riding Chesney and I got the same tingly feeling in my knickers. I came then, and right now I'm coming...oh my god! I'm coming on Knox's face. My whole lower body is trembling, my thighs shaking, pulsing as I let go, screaming out, "Oh god! Knox!"

He again takes my hips in his strong grip, pushing me back to sit on his abs instead. His face is coated in my come. And he licks his lips, moaning.

"Fuck, Dakota," he says, raspy.

I lean down to kiss him, licking my come off his face as well.

I don't know who I am right now, because I'm being a very dirty, bad girl. But I don't care because being with Knox like this feels incredible.

"I want to have sex with you, Knox," I announce, after breaking the kiss.

"Soon, kitten," he promises, giving me a peck of a kiss.

I don't like that reaction. It makes me question everything we've done so far. Makes me question if he really does want me.

"Do you want to have sex with me?" I ask, pushing out my chest as I sit up.

"Of course kitten," he admits, reaching down between us to touch my sensitive spot. "But not until you're eighteen."

"That's ages away," I huff at him annoyed. "Can I do something else for you, in the meantime?" I let the question fall from my mouth, hoping he won't say no when he actually hears what I want to do.

Take My Heart

"Like what kitten?" he questions, with his sexy smirk again.

"Suck your dick," I blurt out, feeling a blush colour my cheeks. "I've been watching things about it in my bedroom at night."

"Not now, kitten," he says, shaking his head. "What you've done tonight is beyond amazing."

I kiss him, hard.

"Fine Dr Ellersan, but when I do that I'm going to blow your mind."

He chuckles again, the vibrations making me tingle again.

"I don't doubt that kitten."

"Why are you calling me kitten?" I blurt out the question I've been wondering since the first time he called me that.

He kisses me again, taking my breath away. And then he whispers to me in the sexy, gruff voice, "Because you purr for me, Dakota."

"That's dirty Dr Ellersan," I tease, my lips just a breath away from his.

"You, my kitten make me a very dirty man," he admits in his sexy voice before he kisses me again. "And if you don't head home now like a good girl I won't be keeping my promise to you tonight."

I laugh, then huff as I climb off his lap.

"I don't really want you to keep that promise," I admit because it's true. I want to have sex with him, like right now, yesterday, not tomorrow, or in a couple of months when I'm eighteen.

"I know Dakota, but I need to. We've moved really fast, and I can't take advantage of you any more than I already have."

I don't feel like he's taken advantage of me, but things definitely have moved fast. And maybe I'm not ready yet, because even though he'll be gentle like he already has I'm scared about having sex for the first time.

I nod, admitting out loud, "I know."

He watches me then as I get dressed, and sits up on the couch. He stands to give me a deep kiss before I leave his apartment, with my heart on fire for him. Things definitely changed tonight.

As I get in the car I text Ava.

Bestie, you home?

Yeah, Kota. Come over.

Once at Ava's she ushers me inside, smiling the entire time as we head up to her room. Sitting down in the beanbags on her bedroom floor, Ava can't stop smiling at me when she blurts out, "Kota, you're glowing. What happened?"

"I...I've been really dirty with Knox," I admit, dropping my gaze from my best friend and feeling myself blush.

"How dirty?" Ava asks excitedly. "Did you lose your v?"

Take My Heart

"No...but he's licked me down there twice, and I touched his dick."

I look up at my best friend, even though I'm embarrassed.

"Did he give you Aussie kisses?"

"Yeah," I admit, blushing even more when I think about Knox kissing me there and how I rode his face earlier. "Is that what it's called?"

"Yeah, Kota," Ava says with a smile. "Anything else happen?"

I nod.

"He took me on a date tonight, and then that happened," I tell her, gulping when I continue, "But tonight I also kinda rubbed myself on his dick. And he nearly went inside me."

"Oh gosh, Kota. That's really hot."

"Yep, but he won't take my v," I admit with an annoyed huff that makes Ava laugh. "He wants to wait until I'm eighteen."

"Oh, yeah I guess that's fair enough," Ava says, laughing when she adds, "At least he's giving you orgasms though."

"Yeah, gosh, A. I've never felt something so damn incredible."

"I know Kota," my best friend says with a laugh. "And I'm really happy for you. You're becoming a woman."

We laugh together. And I ask nervously, "Does sex really hurt? Like the first time?"

Caz May

"Yeah, Kota, it does," she tells me with a sad tone. "But I'm sure when it does happen with Knox he'll be really sweet and gentle."

"I hope so. I really want to do it, but I am scared," I divulge, nervously rubbing my hands together.

"I know. I regret my first time," Ava confesses.

"Why?" I question, adding, "I thought Zeke would've made it amazing for you."

Ava drops her head.

"I didn't lose my virginity to Zeke," she mutters, not looking up at me.

"Oh?" I stammer, confused and not sure what to say.

"I lost it to Drake."

"Oh gosh, A. I had no idea," I say, annoyed with myself. "I'm sorry you couldn't talk to me about it. I'm such a prude."

"It's ok, Kota," she tells me with a soft laugh before she teases me, "And you're definitely not a prude now, missy."

"I know. I'm glad I've waited for Knox," I confess with a smile I can't help when I add, "I think he's the one."

"Are you in love with him?"

"Yeah, A. I think I'm in love with him," I acknowledge, nodding.

"That's great, Kota," Ava says standing up and hugging me.

"I better get home, before dad is grounding me," I say pulling back from the hug.

Take My Heart

"Yeah, I can't keep being your scapegoat," Ava jeers, laughing as I leave.

Driving home I'm feeling incredibly happy.

Tonight was beyond incredible and I want to tell Knox I love him. I can only hope that when I do he tells me he loves me back, and we go all the way.

Caz May

Thirty One

Knox

*T*he last months have been a blur, busy in the clinic by day, and spending nights with Dakota in my arms.

I hadn't hidden our relationship from Andrea, as she'd seen Dakota leaving in the morning in her school uniform. Admittedly she looks sexy as hell in her short school skirt, and white button up shirt, and blazer. Coupling it with knee high socks is every man's fantasy, mine included.

Take My Heart

Today, it's been busy, and I've not seen Dakota for about a week. She'd told me there was lots to do on the farm, and her parents were away at a farming conference in the city. I'm a little concerned for her that they'd leave her alone to take care of things around the farm, and to also look after her younger siblings. But she assured me it wasn't the first time.

Even so she'd asked me to come out to the farm to help with something to do with the horses.

After driving in the open gate I park near the house, getting out of the car and heading to the paddock where I saw Dakota on the tractor. Stopping it, she leaps off when she sees me walking towards her.

As she climbs out the hem of her jumper gets caught on the gear knob and re-engages the tractor. She slips, and is pulled under the moving tractor, falling to the ground with a scream.

It's all in slow motion.

I'm watching it unfold, feeling dread and panic rushing through me.

Rushing towards her, I'm fuming that my feet are not pushing me fast enough. And I'm calling out her name in panic as she's trying to get away from the moving tractor.

I reach Dakota, and she lets out an extreme scream just as the wheel hits her leg crushing it, and breaking it.

Reaching into the tractor I yank back on the gear stick, bringing the tractor to a sudden halt.

Caz May

There is blood everywhere and Dakota is clutching her leg, screaming when I pull her back. Her leg is at a weird angle, bone sticking out, and there's a deep large gash on her shoulder, her light jumper ripped to shreds.

Kneeling beside Dakota, I pull out my phone from my back pocket, calling an ambulance. I don't like their response, telling me they're going to be an hour. She doesn't have an hour, and I feel somewhat responsible for this accident.

Tearing my shirt off, I fix her up, wrapping the flannel fabric around her leg to stop the bleeding. I don't have anything to cover the gash on her back, but it's not bleeding near as much as her leg.

"Kitten, I'm going to pick you up now to take you to the hospital," I say impassively, surprised my voice is not quivering. "Is that ok?"

She nods, whimpering slightly. It breaks my heart, but picking her up, I cradle her in my arms, carrying her to my ute.

Putting her in the back seat, I buckle the seat belt over her stomach and get into the drivers seat, gunning it to the hospital so fast a trail of dust follows me.

Halfway into town, I hear the sirens, and see the lights as the police car comes up behind me, indicating for me to pull over. Slipping onto the side of road, I stop the car, rolling the window down. The sergeant by the name of Kent according to his badge eyes.

Take My Heart

"Arvo, Dr Ellersan, any reason for your excessive speeding today?"

"I was just out at the Neelson's farm, and Dakota had an accident. The ambo's were going to be at least an hour," I inform him, trying to keep my tone in check.

I roll the window down, and he glances in at Dakota in agony on my backseat.

"I really don't think we've got time to waste in getting her to the hospital." I'm really angry and frustrated that the Sargeant is taking his time, as we honestly have no time to waste. I don't want the girl I'm falling in love with to bleed out on my back seat, because of me.

"Yes, Dr Ellersan, you're right. Follow me in to town, I'll give you a police escort."

I nod, and he gets back into his car behind me, signalling to get back onto the road.

Thankful for the escort, we get to the hospital in record time, and Dakota is rushed into the ER when we arrive. I want to go with her, be by her side, but all I'm able to do is give her a soft kiss on the forehead as I'm pushed away because I'm not family.

I wanted to call out, 'I love you' as she was hastily wheeled away, but the words caught on my tongue. I can only hope she pulls through the surgery on her leg, and I get to see her and tell her in person.

The idea of losing her has cemented my feelings for her.

Caz May

I'm in love with Dakota Neelson. And when she's out of surgery, I'm going to show her just how much.

Take My Heart

Thirty Two

Dakota

Waking up, my head is foggy giving me a disorientated feeling.

I can't move, pinned to the bed by a multitude of cords leaving my body, and a heavy, ankle to thigh cast is on my right leg.

The door of the room I'm in swings open, with a doctor coming in. Behind him I can see my parents, with my younger brother and sister beside them, but my eyes don't stay on them as sitting on a chair with his head in his

Caz May

hands is Knox. He looks distraught, in another world and it hurts my heart. I'm not feeling much pain so some of the cords must be giving me painkillers, but I can still feel the heartache, Knox's pain becoming mine.

The doctor is in the room now, checking my chart, whilst my parents and siblings fuss around me.

"Lovely to see you awake, Dakota," the doctor says with a smile. His name label says, 'Dr Findley' and I give him a smile that hurts my cheeks when I realise it's Ariel's dad.

"thanks , Dr Findley."

"Do you remember what happened?"

I shake my head. It still feels fuzzy.

"The last thing I remember was being on the tractor, and seeing Knox pull up in his ute."

"You don't recall the accident? Breaking your leg?"

"No, not really. I just feel fuzzy, and my leg and shoulder are throbbing, but aren't painful."

"Well, that's understandable. You're lucky to still have your leg, quite frankly."

I gasp, and so does mum. She's standing by my bed, holding Nebraska and Montana's hands in hers, softly sobbing. Dad is standing behind her, offering comfort to her. I'm so glad to see them, but I want Knox in the room with me too.

"Um, so how bad was it? And my shoulder?"

"Your entire lower leg was shattered. You have a metal plate linking the bones to help them heal, which will take eight weeks in the cast. And then you'll need rehab for at least two weeks."

"Oh, that's a lot. Will I have to stay in here the whole time?"

"We'd recommended that, so we can monitor your pain and healing easily."

It sounds like hell, and I'm worried about school with exams coming up. Also my shoulder is hurting and it's my writing hand.

"Oh, so what about school?"

"That will all be taken care of. You'll be given special consideration for any work or exams you can't complete."

"Ok, thanks, Doctor Findley. What happened with my shoulder?"

"We're not really sure. Possibly a large stick caused a deep gash from your shoulder to just above your hips that needed stitches."

"Oh gosh, no wonder it hurts."

"Are you in pain, sweetheart?" Mum asks me, concern on her face as her gaze drops to me and then up to Dr Findley.

Again I shake my head.

"No, I'm not in pain, but I um...want to see someone else."

"Dr Ellersan?" Doctor Findley asks, adding, "He's been here all night pacing the room, waiting for you to get out of surgery and wake up."

My heart leaps at that. But falls when I glance at my dad as he steps closer to the door. He's raging with anger.

"Has he taken advantage of you, Dakota?"

Anger floods my body. I want to leap off the bed, and scream at dad for even thinking Knox would do that.

"No, he hasn't dad. I...we've been together, yes, but I wanted it."

He raises his hand, stepping closer to the bed, as though he wants to slap me but he tamps the anger down.

Doctor Findley interrupts, "I'll leave you to chat. Press the buzzer if you need anything Dakota."

I nod, smiling at him as he leaves, keeping the door ajar.

Mum is glaring at me, and then at dad. I get the sense I'm in big trouble about what's happened with Knox. But I don't care. I'm in love with him, and I'm only a couple of weeks away from being eighteen. I can make my own decisions.

"What do you mean you wanted it?" Dad questions, indicating to mum to take my siblings out of the room.

She leads Nebraska and Montana out of the room, and Dad clutches the end of the bed in his white knuckles, probing me, "Well, Dakota?"

"In that way, daddy. We've kissed and touched each other."

"I'm not happy about this Dakota. He's a lot older than you."

Take My Heart

"I know that daddy. But that doesn't change how I feel about him. Or how I think he feels about me."

I've never spoken to my dad this way. It's exhilarating.

"We'll talk more about this when you're feeling better."

I scoff, without meaning to. "Can I see him now, please?" I beg.

Dad doesn't say anything, just leaves the room. I can hear voices outside the door for a moment before Knox rushes into the room.

"Oh, kitten. I'm so sorry. Are you ok?"

I nod, smiling at him. My heart is pounding, and I'm feeling tingly down below. I'm in a hospital gown, and not wearing underwear. I could tease Knox and tell him that, but he looks too concerned about me, and it's not really appropriate for the hospital.

"Yes, Dr Ellersan, I'm fine. Thanks to you I'm guessing."

"Yeah, I don't want to tell you what happened, but I'm so glad you're ok Dakota. I was so worried."

"You were worried about me?"

"Yes, kitten. I care about you...I..." He cuts off his words, bending over to kiss me instead of voicing the words I really want to hear him say.

I want to say them too, but instead I kiss him deeper, telling him with my kiss.

I really hope that dad comes around to the idea of Knox and me being together, because I think he's the one for me, and I don't want him to leave my side ever again.

Caz May

Thirty Three

Dakota

Ava is sitting on the edge of my hospital bed, with a smile on her face as she hands me a gift bag with 'Happy 18th' on it.

I wasn't looking forward to my eighteenth birthday, as my parents are always too busy to spend time with me, because my younger siblings are demanding little irrits. I love them, but hate that they're such attention seekers. My parents came into the hospital, but said my present couldn't be wrapped so I've been thinking about that for days.

I honestly just want out of the hospital, out of the cast on my leg as it's so damn itchy it feels like bugs are crawling all over my skin.

Ava's smile drops, even when she says, "Happy birthday, Kota."

I know my expression is downcast, but spending your birthday in hospital sucks.

And also Knox hasn't been in at all this week, and I miss him so much my heart hurts. I haven't told him I love him but I do, so much I feel empty and lost without seeing him. He probably doesn't feel that for me though as he repeatedly—despite what we've done together—tells me I'm too young for him, that we can't be together.

Prying open the gift bag I give my best friend a slight smile, speaking softly, "Thanks, A. It's so pretty."

I pull out the blanket with a horse print on it. It looks like Chesney and it's so plush and soft.

"You're welcome, Kota. I thought you'd love that it looks like Chessie."

"It definitely does," I reply, putting it to my cheek.

"Are you ok, Kota? You seem kinda down," my best friend observes.

I shake my head, looking down at the blanket now in my lap on top of the hospital sheets.

"Not really. I haven't seen Knox all week. I think he's avoiding seeing me."

Caz May

Ava frowns, mirroring my mood with her expression.

"I'm sure he has a reason, Kota."

"Yeah, like he's just used me," I reply in a huff, pulling the blanket up to my cheeks.

"I'm sure it's nothing like that," she assures me. "I meant he's probably just been busy at the clinic."

"Yeah, I guess so," I reply, glancing up at her. "I just feel as though he's just used me for sex." I stumble on the word 'sex', feeling my cheeks colour.

I don't talk about these things with anyone but Ava is my best friend and she's experienced. She's looking at me now, like I've grown two heads, she's that shocked.

"You had sex with him?"

I shake my head, trying not to giggle when I reply, "No, but we've kissed and done other stuff."

"So oral sex?" Ava questions, blinking furiously.

"Yeah that and it's so amazing."

"Yeah, I know," Ava replies adding with a hand on my cast, "and I'm sure Knox is just busy. If he hasn't just jumped into fucking you I think he cares about you and wants you for more than just sex."

"I hope so, A because honestly I don't want another man."

She laughs then, standing up from the bed and singing, "What a man, What a mighty good man."

"Oh yeah, he's a man alright," I singsong back, laughing because my best friend is being silly to lighten the mood.

Take My Heart

Leaning down awkwardly to not get tangled in the wires I still have attached to me, she hugs me.

"I gotta go, Kota, but I hope you've had an ok birthday. We'll party when you can walk."

"Ok, thank you, A. Love you bestie," I say as she walks out.

"Love you back more, bestie," she calls out back, her voice muffled as she bumps into a tall figure coming into the room.

My heart skips. Ava just bumped in him, my man, my Knox. He laughs, his abs vibrating under his tight shirt. And Ava looks at him then at me, mouthing, "definitely a mighty man." She turns on her heels, and leaves with those words hanging in the air.

Knox comes into the room then, grinning.

"Hi kitten." His deep voice sends the tingling to my crotch.

But I'm annoyed at him, for not coming into to see me much at all these last six weeks. He'd said that he cares about me, but he's not shown me that. He hasn't even bought me flowers or anything to brighten this dump of a hospital room. You'd think a man—an older man—would know how to treat a girl, by doing all that kinda of romantic stuff but Knox hasn't done that. I'm doubting my feelings for him—but for only a moment—as he sits on the edge of the bed, his hand reaching forward to cup my cheek in a soft caress.

Caz May

"I've missed you, kitten," he tells me, all husky and sexy. It makes me want to hurl myself across the bed into his lap to kiss him like crazy. My whole body is aching for him, but I can't move an inch, and I groan in annoyance.

I still don't say anything, so Knox speaks again, "Did I hear your friend say it's your birthday?"

"Yeah," I say with a soft voice, nodding as I mutter under my breath, "Not that you'd care."

He scoffs leaning forward, and kissing me on the forehead. It's sweet, but feels forced.

"Of course I care, Dakota. Why didn't you tell me?"

"Because I...I didn't think you'd care. I'm too young for you."

He doesn't reply, only inhales a long hard breath. I feel his exhale fan over my cheeks, and again it makes me groan in frustration because I want his lips on mine, even if it's wrong. But now it's not wrong, as I'm eighteen.

"Dakota...please," Knox says rapsy, edging closer to me on the bed.

"Kiss me, Dr Ellersan," I taunt him. "I'm eighteen now."

"I know, kitten, but we still need to be cautious."

I huff, angrily folding my arms over my chest.

"I don't want to be. I want you Knox."

"I want you too, Dakota, so much, but please...we need to take things slow." He says the words slowly, and then he's kissing me. I give in, because he's kissing me, and I can't resist his kisses, plus I've missed him. Moaning into the kiss, I desperately want to move closer to him but I can't. Curse being here. Curse him pushing me away, even though his lips are still on mine.

I pull back, gasping for a breath. Knox has stolen my air. And the room is stifling.

"I'm sorry, kitten. I'm sorry," he says breathlessly, standing up from the bed. He grabs my hand, kissing the back of it. "I have to go, kitten. I'll come back tomorrow."

I want to hurl angry words at him, but I don't.

"I'm getting my cast off tomorrow."

"That's great, kitten. I'll come see you then."

And before I can reply, he slips out the door, taking my heart with him.

Knox

I'd left Dakota's hospital room yesterday, feeling completely flat. She's eighteen now, so being with her isn't illegal anymore, but I still feel wary.

Partly scared of falling for someone else again after Madison, and also wary of falling for a girl still young and inexperienced. The worry is in my mind that she'll get bored of me, basically use me for my experience—what I can teach her about her body—and then she'll leave me and find someone her age. Madison was a couple years younger than me, and she left me.

Caz May

But something tells me—a sixth sense or something—that Dakota is different. She's mature beyond her years, and sweet, loving. I can tell she doesn't love easily, and she hasn't said the words but I'm sure she's in love with me.

I'm falling for her too. But I know I probably shouldn't.

Clutching the 'Happy 18th' shiny balloon and bunch of flowers in one hand, and the small wrapped present I bought for her on a whim when I saw it in the window at the jewellers on my way back to the clinic—the other day —I push open the door of her hospital room. Her eyes light up the moment she sees it's me, even though the balloon is covering my face. It's possible she's smiling because of the balloon and flowers but when I put them down on the bed, her grin widens.

Leaning down I kiss her forehead. "Happy eighteenth birthday, kitten."

"Thank you, Knox," she replies sweetly, taking the small wrapped present I hand to her as I sit on the edge of the bed.

"Open it, kitten," I coerce softly.

She starts to tear the paper off, her eyes boggling when she glances at the small square velvet box she's now holding.

She looks up at me, tears in the corner of her eyes.

"You didn't have to get me anything, Knox."

"When I saw this the other day, I instantly thought of you. And I had to get it for you."

Flipping open the lid of the box, she shrieks excitedly, "Oh gosh, Knox. I love it!"

Her thumb brushes over the silver bracelet, tracing the dangling paw print charm.

"I'm glad," I admit, thankful my present has made her smile. "You can add other charms to it later."

She leans forward to kiss me, a sweet loving kiss. And she whispers against my lips, "I love y...it."

Shocked I break the kiss, glaring at her with a question on the tip of my tongue. I swear she nearly said I love you. But with her kiss against my lips I could've been mistaken.

"When do you get the cast off?" I ask instead.

"Not sure," she replies, her head down. "Hopefuly by the end of the day. Once it's done, they said I can be discharged in a week if rehab goes well."

"That's great kitten," I say, caressing her cheek with the back of my hand. "Do you want me to come and pick you up? Or help you with rehab?"

"Could you? My parents are still out of town."

"Of course, kitten, " I tell her, kissing her again. "Let me know when I need to be here."

"Thank you."

I give her a smile, and say, "I have to go now though. Lots of animals to see today at the clinic."

"That's ok, Dr Ellersan," she taunts. "Go be a super vet."

She giggles, and standing from the bed I give her a final kiss.

Caz May

"I'll see you soon, kitten."

I almost let the words 'I love you' slip from my mouth, even though I'm not sure a hundred percent if I feel them for her just yet.

Leaving though, I know she has taken a piece of my heart.

Thirty Four

Knox

*H*olding Dakota around the waist, I keep her steady as she grips the bars on the walking frame. She groans in frustration as she tries to take a step forward.

"I can't do it!" She screams, starting to sob.

"It's ok, kitten. Take it slow," I comfort, kissing her temple. "I'm here. I won't let you fall."

Caz May

She turns to look at me, the corner of her mouth curling in a smile.

"Promise?"

"I promise kitten. You can do it."

She lets out a squeak of a laugh, giving me a kiss that makes my heart race.

Again Dakota groans, steadily moving forward. One step, then two. Three.

"That's it, kitten, keep going," I encourage. "You can do this, sweetheart."

She moans at my new endearing nickname for her, and edges on, moving along the walking frame with determination until she reaches the end.

"Knox!"she screams excitedly, turning around in my embrace, and nearly stumbling. I catch her as she falls against my chest. "I did it!" She beams at me.

"Yeah you did, kitten. I'm so proud of you."

I kiss her then, a deeply sensual kiss. And when she breaks it, looking up at me with hooded eyes those words are on the tip of my tongue. Those three words that I've been so close to telling her since the accident.

"I know. I can't believe i got to the end."

"Yeah, maybe tomorrow you can try without my help."

"That would be amazing," Dakota beams, dropping her hands from the bar and taking a couple steps backwards. She's holding up her leg, not letting her foot rest on the ground, still hesitating in putting pressure on it.

Take My Heart

I step closer to her, not actually fully embracing her but ready to grab her if she falls.

"Does it hurt kitten?" I ask her.

She nods, wincing as she moves closer to me.

"Yes," she hisses. "It's aching."

"Aww, kitten. I'm sorry, sweetheart, but it will get better and easier. I promise."

"I know," she affirms.

"Come on, let's go back to your room and do some stretches."

She smiles at me, cheekily saying, "Ok."

Reaching out she grabs my hand and I gently tug her to my side.

"Lean on me sweetheart," I tell her, taking slow steps out of the rehab room.

"Thank you, Knox," she whispers softly, tightening her grip on my waist as she stretches up on her good leg to press a soft kiss to my cheek.

"You don't have to thank me for this, or anything kitten," I inform her, kissing her temple and mumbling, "I I...care about you." I nearly let those three words slip from my mouth without thinking. I feel them for her, without a doubt I'm in love with her. But feeling the words and verbalising them are two very different things.

The look Dakota is giving me as we hobble back to her room tells me she knows exactly what I was about to say.

She stays silent though until we reach her room and she sits on the edge of the creaky hospital bed. She sighs

Caz May

deeply, shifting on the bed from side to side, her fingers gripping the edge when she glances up at me. Her expression is downcast.

"I...love you, Knox," she murmurs, her eyes not leaving mine.

I pull her into a hug, and she starts to sob into my chest. I stroke her hair, the words caught in my throat, causing me to grunt in panic.

Dakota pulls back from the hug, looking up at me with eyes full of tears and streaked cheeks. I've hurt her by my lack of words after her confession to me.

"I...care about you sweetheart. I really do," I stammer, stumbling over my response as thoughts of the past fill my head. I need to explain to her why I can't verbalise my feelings for her. Why I can't get the word love to leave my mouth, even though I do love her. I'm just not ready to say it.

"Don't you love me?" She stammers, sniffing back her tears.

"I...well, I haven't told you but the last time I felt the way I do about you, I was left at the altar."

Dakota gasps.

"Oh, I'm sorry. That's so cruel," she says angrily, adding a calmer question, "who would do that to you?" She's shaking her head in disbelief.

"I thought I loved her, and she loved me, as she'd told me but it was all a lie to get my money. To get an in with my father.

"I can't take the risk with my heart, kitten. Please...i just can't do that yet. Her betrayal and contempt still weigh on me."

Dakota nods, smiling.

"I'm sorry someone you loved hurt you. But I won't. You're the only man for me. I know it."

I don't reply to that, instead I kiss her softly, standing up after to grab the resistance band from the chair opposite the bed. Handing it to her, she huffs in annoyance.

"Do I have to?"

"Yes, kitten, you need to stretch."

"Fine," she huffs again, grabbing the resistance band and hooking it around the base of her foot. Kneeling behind her I encourage her as she stretches, arching her foot back and forth, and bending her knee. When she groans loudly—in pain—I hug her from behind and she drops the band on he floor. Turning back to me, we kiss. She shows me her sweet, all consuming love for me in her kisses, and reluctantly I pull back.

"You did fabulous today, kitten," I tell her, smiling. "They might let you out soon."

Scooting back on the bed she laughs. "I hope so. I'm going crazy in here. I miss you."

"How can you miss me when you see me nearly everyday?" I question, knowing exactly what she means but wanting to hear her say it.

Caz May

"I miss our naughty naked touching," she confesses, a soft blush colouring her cheeks. She's so unbelievably beautiful.

"I know kitten," I reply nodding and smiling. "We'll get to do that soon, but you have to be strong and get out of here first."

Her smile is wide then, as I give her a final kiss before I go.

All I can think about as I drive home is the look in her eyes when she confessed her love to me. I'm an idiot for not saying it back, because even though she kissed me after and clearly still wants to be with me I know my idiocy of not being able to say it back has hurt her. I've hurt the girl I'm in love with it, and that hurts like the pain I felt watching Madison running back down the aisle.

With a busy week in the clinic I haven't had a chance to go in to see Dakota, and help with the final few days of rehab.

I honestly miss the girl, so when my phone vibrates in my jeans pocket, I yank it out excitedly.

The message is from Dakota.

Miss you, Dr Ellersan.

Take My Heart

Her teasing side is out to play. She only ever calls me Dr Ellersan when she's being naughty, and I'll probably never tell her that it turns me on. It sounds so dirty when she purrs that in her sweet voice.

Is that so, kitten?

I text back, with a grin on my face.

Yes, I'm not wearing knickers under my gown now.

God, help me. I'm thinking of my girl in a hospital bed, of her wearing no underwear and touching herself.

Are you touching yourself, kitten?

Would be naughty if you were

The three little dots appear on the screen, and then disappear a moment, only to reappear for a second before her message pops up, shocking me.

Yes, dr ellersan. I'm touching my pussy under the covers whilst I'm thinking about you

Fuck me dead. Now I'm sporting a hard on--in the middle of the damn day--in the clinic when I have patients who I need to attend to.

I want to yank my damn dick out and jerk off like a pubescent schoolboy. That's what she does to me, and even though I shouldn't, and shouldn't encourage her I dial her number.

Caz May

I barely have a second to get my dick out of my jeans, as she answers almost immediately.

"Hello, Dr Ellersan," she purrs into the phone.

"Hello, kitten," I reply back, huskily as I fist my aching dick in my hand.

"You made my dick hard, kitten," I inform her, starting to stroke myself, and groaning with the words.

"I'm wet for you, Dr Ellersan," she murmurs, her breath hitching.

"Are you touching yourself for me, kitten?" I question, stroking my dick harder just thinking about her wet pussy. It's been too long since we've been together beyond kissing and I'm so pent up with lust for her.

"Yes, Dr Ellersan. I want to make you come, whilst I come for you."

"Fuck, Dakota," I curse out. "I'm in the fucking clinic right now. God!"

"Mmm, are you touching your dick?" she asks, innocence in her voice.

"Fuck, yes, I am, Dakota," I scream out, stroking my dick fiercely and shooting ropes of come over the examination table.

I hear her giggle on the line. "Did you just come everywhere, Dr Ellersan?"

"Yes, kitten," I taunt. "Now it's your turn. I'm not hanging up until I hear you moan for me, sweetheart."

Her breath hitches again, and she starts panting.

"Does it feel good, kitten?"

Take My Heart

"Yes," she hisses. "But your hand, and mouth feels better, Dr Ellersan."

"Oh I bet, kitten. Imagine it's me touching you, and licking you. I love making you come for me."

"Mmm," she moans loudly, a gasp escaping her lips when I hear a loud banging.

"Oh shit," she stammers. "The doctor is here, I gotta go."

I hear her hang up, and laugh at her being caught in the act. My poor girl.

Tucking my dick back into my jeans, I type her another text,

You got caught huh, kitten?

Yes, I didn't get to come

I'll make you come more than once when I pick you up tomorrow

You better x

I'm startled then, almost dropping my phone when there's a knock on the exam room door, and it opens slightly. Andrea's head pops in and she glances around, looking at the exam table covered in my come. I swear I blush, as she does.

"Um, sorry to bother you, Knox, but there's an emergency just come in." Her voice stumbles on the word 'come', her eyes still on the exam table.

"No worries, Andrea. I'll just be a minute," I inform her, nodding towards my mess. "Could you get them set up in room one, instead?"

"No worries. You ok?"

"Yeah, just need to finally make Dakota mine when I pick her up tomorrow."

Andrea smiles at me, leaning on the door.

"You love her, don't you?"

"Yeah, I do. She makes me feel like a kid again, in a good way."

"That's great. I'm glad to hear it. I'll see you in room one, when you're ready."

She heads out of the room, and I grab a cloth, wetting it in the sink and wiping it over the exam table to clean off my come.

I'm lucky to have Andrea as my vet nurse, and friend. She tells it like it is, and never judges me. And I have my Dakota, as well. I can't wait to have all of her, to tell her that I love her with all my heart. She's the only girl for me, without a doubt I let her take my heart months ago, from the very first words out of her mouth. It's just taken my mind a little longer to catch up.

Take My Heart

Thirty Five

Knox

Much to Dakota's annoyance, she'd had to stay in hospital for a couple more weeks after getting her cast off. Rehab had been a slow process, and even now a few weeks down the track she was still healing and was going to have to wear a moon-boot.

Since last night when we finished our phone sex conversation, this time using FaceTime I'm eager to pick her up, so I can finally make her mine completely. I'd come right out and told her that I want to sleep with her, and her whole face lit up with delight.

Heading into the hospital to discharge her I can't stop grinning, holding another bunch of flowers for her.

When I get to the room, she's standing, leaning on the edge of the bed. She smiles at me, then pouts, being all cute.

"I've been waiting for you, Knox," she huffs at me. "What took you so long?" She's a bit grumpy.

"I had an emergency at the clinic, kitten, and then I had to get petrol in the Mercedes."

Again she huffs at me grumpily. "Why didn't you bring your other car?"

"Because it's too hard for you to get into with your moon-boot, and limited movement, kitten."

"Fine, but you could've told me you were going to be late."

Truthfully I could've done that, but it doesn't matter as I'm here now, and I'm taking her home.

I chuckle slightly, as she's still pouting.

"If you don't stop being a grumpy kitten, I won't make you come when we get back to your house," I tell her, teasingly giving her a smirk.

"Fine," she huffs, stepping closer to me when she taunts, "I want to come so bad, Dr Ellersan."

I kiss her temple, pulling her against my side as we shuffle out of the room. She signs the discharge papers at the desk, and I take one of her hands as she carefully hobbles out with me to the car.

Opening the passenger door, I help her into the car, rushing around to the driver's side to get in.

My gaze is on her outfit as I start the engine and head out onto the main road. She's still wearing a hospital gown.

"Are you wearing any knickers under that gown, kitten?"

She shakes her head, opening her legs and making the gown hitch up her thighs.

"No, Dr Ellersan," she murmurs, biting down on her lip.

"Fuck, Dakota. Hearing that makes me want to speed to the farm," I say cockily, trying not to actually groan.

"Do it," she taunts with a laugh and cheeky, way to sexy smirk.

"I'd love to kitten, but I can't risk a fine."

She pouts at me, again, huffing, "Fine touch me then, so I'm ready to come when we get home."

Her eyes are on me, desire flashing in them as she taunts me with her gaze that drops to my crotch. My dick is straining against my jeans, painfully so.

Still driving, clutching the wheel tightly with one hand, I reach between her thighs, brushing my fingers up them to her pussy.

She shifts on the seat, closing her legs.

I laugh at her.

Caz May

"Don't you want me to touch you now, kitten?" I taunt her, giving her a wink as I turn my head towards her for a moment.

"I do, but I'll come on your seat," she informs me, her tone not wavering.

I laugh again, jeering, "We can't have that kitten. We'll be back at yours soon, and I'll make you come more than once, with my fingers, tongue and deep inside you."

"Hurry up then," she pleads eagerly.

I floor the Mercedes, hitting one-thirty, not caring anymore about a speeding fine. Dust kicks up behind the car when we reach the farm and drive through the open gate.

Momentarily I wonder if any animals have escaped with the gate being open, but Dakota doesn't seem fazed, and the only animal that needs release now is me.

Dakota

Opening my car door, I'm about to get out when I hear Knox grunt from beside me angrily.

"Wait, kitten," he grunts, opening his door and getting out.

Take My Heart

Before I can move again, put my aching ankles on the ground he's at the door, his arms wrapping around me to help me to my feet.

"Let me help you, kitten. Lean on me," he says, calmly but with a glint in his eyes.

He's just as eager to get inside and get naughty together as I am. I've soaked the back of my hospital gown with my arousal and it's clinging to my butt cheeks.

Carefully with Knox's arm around me and not putting too much weight on my foot we hobble inside. The door is unlocked, and I panic a moment thinking my parents and my younger siblings are home, but the house is quiet.

"You ok, kitten?" Knox asks, kissing my temple.

"Yeah, I just thought my parents were home for a second."

"Oh, are you expecting them soon?"

"No, not until tomorrow," I tell him, shifting out of his arms and hobbling down the hallway to my room. He rushes after me, and stands in my doorjamb staring at me with lust flaring in his eyes.

Dr Ellersan wants me, and I want him. I want to be his naughty kitten. It's a silly nickname, but I love it when he calls me that. It's cute, but dirty. And I love being dirty with Knox. No guy—man—has ever given me the butterflies in my belly and my lower body like he does. Ava would think she had a completely different person for a best friend if she knew about the thoughts—and things—I've thought about and done with Knox.

Caz May

With the way he's standing in the doorframe just now, I'm desperate for him to make me come. I can feel my arousal dripping down my thighs, I'm that turned on for the gorgeous man in front of me. The gorgeous man who has taken my heart. I think he feels the same, but he's scared to love me, love anyone. I can only hope that when we take the next step—in mere minutes, hopefully—that he'll realise he loves me as well. I'm about to give the man my virginity, and I'm nervous but at the same time I'm not.

To tease him, I smirk as I bend down and grip the hem of the hospital gown in my fingers. Taking in a deep breath, I slowly lift it up, exposing more of my naked body as I take it off, and throw it aside. His eyes darken and he groans, crossing the threshold into my room, stalking towards me as his gaze drinks me in.

"Fuck, Dakota, you're breathtakingly beautiful." He kisses me, not letting me reply as he steals my words, and my breath. The kiss is hungry, needy and possessive, but sweet as his tongue licks over my lips, begging for more. I give him more, teasing him by darting my tongue out to meet his, which causes him to groan and pull back from the kiss.

He lifts his t-shirt over his head, and even though I've seen him naked before I gasp from getting a glimpse of his abs that are smothered with light blonde hair. It makes him look more manly, older and very sexy. Stepping closer to him I grab the waistband of his jeans, tugging him towards me, as I stumble back towards my bed.

We fall against it and I pull him down with me, our bodies colliding and then our lips meet in a hot possessive kiss.

He pulls back again, taking my breath away when he starts to lave kisses over my boobs, completely taking one into his hot mouth and biting the nipple, before soothing the sting with his tongue. The sensation causes my hips to buck up against his, a moan falling from my lips with his name, "Knox."

Stopping the sweet torture he gazes at me, a glint in his eyes, a look of pure adoration. I've never felt more beautiful.

"What do you want, kitten?" he questions me, his tone husky.

"For you to take me, Knox," I reply brazenly.

"Are you sure Dakota?"

"Yes, Knox. I want you to fuck me."

He groans then, wordlessly leaning over me again, this time parting my legs with a firm grip on my thighs. He's staring between my legs, and bites his lip a moment.

"Your pussy is so pretty, kitten," he murmurs with that same husky tone. It makes my 'pussy' pulse, and throb because I'm so turned on from his words, and what he does to me.

I can't even say anything in response before he drops to his knees, and his head is between my thighs. His

Caz May

tongue darts out, licking my pussy, and I moan loudly, grabbing his hair in my fists as his tongue teases me. I've never had anyone else do this to me, but I'm sure Knox is an expert, because it's only mere minutes before I'm pushing and bucking against his face, an orgasm hitting me hard.

My hands drop from his hair to my sides, and gripping the sheets I tremble from the orgasm. Knox stands, watching me as he undoes his belt, and his jeans, dropping them to floor. His dick is straining against the front of his jocks and his thick thighs are pulsing with the tension in his body.

"Are you sure you want this, kitten?" he asks, cupping his length in his hand.

"Yes, Knox," I reply teasingly, sitting up and reaching out to grab his erection. He groans, and then gasps when I shove his jocks down. Stepping out of them he leans down, cupping my cheeks and kissing me, whilst I stroke his dick, causing it to harden even more in my hands.

With a moan he breaks the kiss, glaring at me forlorn.

"Kitten, we need protection," he muses, kissing my forehead. "I'm not taking your innocence away without keeping you safe."

Annoyed I grunt, shifting on the bed and getting up without saying anything. I probably shouldn't even be considering sneaking into my parents room, about to rifle through my dad's drawer for a condom. I shouldn't even know they're in his underwear drawer, but I'd found them

Take My Heart

one day when I was putting laundry away. I'd cringed at the thought of my parents having sex, because eww…but now I'm grateful that the condoms are still there in the drawer as I slide it out slowly. Thankfully the date is still valid as well I notice as I take one from the box, careful to put it back exactly as I found it.

I'd be truly mortified if dad found out. I wouldn't be his innocent little girl anymore.

Rushing back into my room, I skid across the floor back to the bed, throwing the condom to Knox with a giggle.

"Where did you get this, kitten?" Knox asks as he catches the condom.

"Doesn't matter, Knox," I taunt him, sitting on the edge of my bed. "Put it on, and fuck me."

He groans again, in that sexy manly way. And stepping in between my legs he carefully tears open the foil, taking out the condom and rolling it down his dick from the tip.

Leaning over me, he caresses my cheek, murmuring, "Are you sure, kitten?"

"Yes, Knox. I want you inside me," I tell him, cupping his cheeks and bringing his face to mine to kiss him.

I can feel the tip of his dick brushing against my clit, and pushing my hips up to encourage him I yelp as he slips inside me, slowly. It hurts.

Knox edges further inside me, cupping my cheeks when he softly asks, "Dakota, you ok? Does it hurt?"

"Yes, but please, keep going."

Caz May

Slowly he pushes further inside me, and again it hurts but only for a moment. Knox leans over to kiss me, starting to rock his hips, his dick moving in and out of my body.

Looking up at him, breaking the kiss I murmur softly, "I love you, Knox. Thank you for this."

He groans, seeming shocked by my words. "Don't, Dakota. Don't thank me for taking your virginity."

I don't have any words. I just wrap my arms around his back, my legs around his butt, and pull him in, deeper.

The pain is gone, pleasure overtaking me as Knox thrusts in and out, grunting and panting as his pace increases.

He stills a moment, and I can feel his dick throbbing inside me as he gets closer to release.

He thrusts one last time, calling out, "Fuck, kitten. Fuck, I love you."

My insides feel warm, and he collapses on my chest a moment, looking at me with adoration in his eyes. He kisses me softly, brushing my hair from my cheeks.

Even though I didn't come again, I feel satisfied. He told me he loves me.

Sliding out, he lays down beside me and pulls me into his arms, kissing me again. I want to hear him say it again, to know that he means it.

"Do you really love me?"

He looks at me, staring right into my eyes, his hand brushing against my pussy. A finger slips inside, and he murmurs, "Yes, Dakota, I love you."

"I love you, too, Dr Ellersan," I reply, a hint of teasing in my voice. "And that feels good."

"Really, kitten? You want to come again?"

"Yes," I hiss through my teeth, as his finger caresses me, sending me to the brink again.

Knox kisses my forehead, and whispers, "Come with my finger fucking you this time, but next time, kitten I'll make you come with my cock buried deep inside your pretty pussy."

Those sexy, dirty words are enough to make me clench around him, my lower body trembling as I let go again. I scream his name, another amazing orgasm hitting me, all over his fingers. He pulls them out, and puts them up to my lips. I lick them and then kiss him, rolling over so I'm on top of him.

"Is next time now?"

He chuckles softly, his hands on my hips as he pulls me down for a kiss.

"No, kitten, you'll be too sore if I have my way with you again," he tells me in an authoritative tone. "But soon, I promise. I'm not letting you get away."

"I'm not letting you go either, Dr Ellersan. I love you, too much."

Caz May

"I love you too, Dakota," he replies, sitting up with me still in his lap. "I really should get going soon, and you should get some rest."

I give him a kiss, and say teasingly, "Yes, doctor."

He stands, gripping my hips to lift me with him.

Our lips find each other again, in another sweet kiss. And turning us around he puts me down on the bed, pulling the sheets back so I can get comfy.

I close my eyes, drifting in and out of sleep. Knox doesn't leave, except to discard of the condom, and I hear him putting his boxers back on before he gets into bed with me, pulling me close as we both drift to sleep.

I will never forget this night. And I can't wait to tell Ava.

Thirty Six

Knox

After tucking Dakota into bed, after laying with her in my arms until dusk I'm driving home, thinking about her, and what we just shared.

She gave me her virginity, and she's given me her heart as well. The smile on her face when I told her I love her is one I'll never forget. And honestly I hope I'll get to see a smile like that many times.

Caz May

I'd never dreamt of falling in love again, but there's something about Dakota and her sweet innocence, but maturity at the same time. It was easy to fall in love with her and she's easy to love.

I'm sure as hell not second guessing how she feels about me either. It's clear she loves me too, and I've never been sure of that before.

Getting home, my house feels lonely even with Toby greeting me eagerly.

Ruffling his fur, I admit to him, "I told her Tobes."

He barks loudly at me in response, following me as I head to the bathroom.

I've confided in my dog a lot these past few months, telling him how I was feeling about Dakota from that very first day she walked into the clinic. And the big doofus fell for my girl from the moment he met her too. I'd never believed in love at first sight, or any of that bullshit, but I think I did fall for Dakota from the first time we interacted. She's beguiling, and beautifully carefree.

In the bathroom I strip from my jeans, and shirt, sniffing the shirt a moment to inhale the smell of Dakota's jasmine perfume lingering on it. It sends my head into a spin, drawing my dick to attention. I'm a hundred percent in love with her when just a hint of her scent has me hard, and wishing I could rush back to her house again to be with her again. Sleeping with her wasn't mind blowing, but it was arresting in the way it made me feel.

Take My Heart

Stupidly I wasn't going to admit my feelings for her right after taking her virginity but holding her close afterwards the words fell from my lips, and I know it was the right thing to do.

With how responsive and eager to learn Dakota is, the sex will get better, and with her it's more than that. She's taken my heart, and with it my body which is responding now to thoughts of her as I step into the shower.

Slowly I start stroking my dick with one hand, using the other to steady myself against the wall.

Closing my eyes, I continue stroking my length, thinking of Dakota moaning my name as I stripped her of every shred of her innocence and made her mine completely. The shower is filling with steam, and the smell of jasmine is wafting into the space, from her scent that has lingered on my skin.

My dick throbs in my hand, and with a final stroke, her name a loud roar from my mouth I come, spurting come all over the shower walls. I'm well and truly gone, for Dakota Abigail Neelson. It might be crazy, but holy crap, I'm in love, and I'm going to marry her.

Caz May

Thirty Seven

Dakota

When I had the accident and found myself lying in a hospital bed, unable to move I didn't think I'd be able to go to Graduation.

Truly I thought I'd be failing and repeating year twelve, but I'm not. I can't believe I'm at my high school graduation after just getting out of hospital a month ago.

The whole ceremony was a blur. I only really paid attention to my friends going up, and my dufus of a

Take My Heart

younger brother getting their diploma's. Speaking of Braeden, he's been over at ours a bit in the last month, mainly for dinner but he's also been having hushed conversations with mum, and my older sister Georgia. She's back living at home, after she broke up with her boyfriend, and has subsequently sworn off men. She'd jokingly—I think—told me she was going to become a lesbian and pash her best friend Florence, but I'm doubting that. It had been good to have Georgia home though, chatting all night with her lying in the bed across from me. It was just like old times, and I'd really missed having my older sister around. I'd told her all about Knox, and losing my virginity to him. She praised me, teased me that I was finally a woman, and we broke into a fit of crazy laughter.

Georgia certainly doesn't act her age, being twenty seven. She's closer in age to Knox, but she also promised she wouldn't steal my man. And I honestly don't think she could. Knox has shown he's smitten with me, showering me with affection and thoughtful actions like taking me out on cute dates, and giving me flowers every time he sees me. I practically spend every waking hour with him. And wish I could spend every night with him too.

After seeing Ava and Ariel with their boys I hobble over to them, trying not to wince when I step on my foot. I probably shouldn't have worn heels, but I liked how they looked and didn't think wearing my fancy cowboy boots to graduation was appropriate.

My friends smile at me, and Ariel asks keenly, "Are you coming to Drake's after party?"

"No, it's not my thing," I reply sadly, as I feel like I'm just making an excuse. "And I'm not really up to it. It's been hard being on my feet all day."

"Yeah, you should get some rest," my best friend says when I feel 'him' behind me.

Dr Ellersan, the man I love is standing behind me.

His arms wrap around my waist, and he steadies me when I stumble on my feet a little. Just having him near effects me, in every way.

"Ready to go, kitten?" he asks in my ear, his breath fanning against my cheek and making me shiver. "Your parents are waiting."

"Yeah," I reply, stepping out of Knox's arms to give hugs to Ava and Ariel.

We quickly say our goodbyes, and I hobble off with Knox holding me around the waist.

"You ok, kitten?" he asks as we get to his car and he helps me into the passenger seat.

"Yeah, just nervous about you officially meeting my parents."

"I'm sure it will be fine, kitten," he assures me as we begin the drive to the farm.

Take My Heart

Mum and Dad had told me some family—and friends—would be over for drinks to celebrate with me, and the thought of sharing that with Knox is making me giddy.

Growing up definitely has some perks. And I'm ready for them all, with the man I love by my side.

Caz May

Thirty Eight

Knox

*T*he entire time we're having dinner and drinks with Dakota's family, back on the farm I'm on edge.

It's an official meeting, but they're all so casual, laughing and including me as I stay glued to my girl's side. I'm hoping they can see I really care about her.

She's yawning, her head resting against my shoulder. I wrap an arm around her waist, smiling when her dad comes towards us, a slight, wavering smile on his lips.

Take My Heart

He nods at me in acknowledgement, outstretching his hand for me to shake.

"Great to meet you, officially, Dr Ellersan," he greets me, speaking really formally.

"Likewise, Mr Neelson. You can call me Knox in this company."

"Thank you, Knox, I appreciate that," he again replies with the same formal tone. I'm clearly not going to be able to call him by his first name—yet—if ever, and I bite my tongue to not say something snarky I'll regret later.

"Also thank you, for everything you did for Dakota with the accident."

"It was nothing. I'd do anything for her," I inform her dad, kissing Dakota's temple, as I think in my head...*I'm in love with her.*

Her dad gives me a nod, heading into the kitchen again.

Dakota yawns again, shifting in my arms and pulling back. She looks up at me, her eyelids droopy.

"You should head to bed, kitten," I say, squaring my hands on her shoulders. "You look beat."

"I am," she meekly says, stifling another yawn. "Can you tuck me in, Dr Ellersan?"

The way she asks that question is so innocent and cute.

"Of course, kitten. Lead the way."

I follow Dakota down the hallway, trying to stop my brain from heading down the path of remembering our first night together.

Dakota doesn't make it easy on me, as she steps into her bedroom, gripping my hand and yanking me in with her. Our bodies collide and I rest my forehead against hers to whisper, "We can't kitten. Your parents are just down the hall."

She stumbles back, bending down to lift off her pretty, very revealing already black dress.

Seeing her standing before me in just lacy black knickers makes me groan, lustfully because damn she's gorgeous, and she's mine. But I can't make her moan in pleasure right now, as much as I want to with her parents' mere metres away.

"I don't care, Dr Ellersan," Dakota states, her voice teasing and childlike. "Kiss me, and tuck me into bed," she continues, holding her still aching ankle up as she steps slowly back towards her bed.

Her nipples have hardened with the cool night breeze billowing through her open window, and also because I'm sure she's turned on with my appreciative gaze of her beautiful body.

"Fuck, Dakota, you're so beautiful," I groan, stepping towards her and kissing her, hard and passionately with my hands cupping her cheeks as I crush my lips to hers. She moans against my mouth, asking for more. Her barely covered pussy is against my aching dick, and I want to

Take My Heart

more than anything to push her down on her bed, and celebrate her graduation with my dick buried deep inside her, but I can hear footsteps coming from down the hallway.

In a panic, I break the kiss.

"Get in bed, kitten. Someone's coming."

She pouts, which of course as always is sexy as hell. And pulling back the covers she slides under them, groaning.

Kissing her forehead and then her lips softly I pull the sheets up to her chin, and smile at her.

"Goodnight, kitten. I love you."

"I love you, too, Knox," she murmurs, her eyes closing as she quickly drifts into sleep.

Sighing deeply I head out of her room, bumping into her dad as he's come to check on her.

He's giving me a glare, telling me without words that he knows what I was doing with his daughter in her bedroom.

Trying to remain calm, as my heart is racing I head back down the hallway, waiting for Mr Neelson to follow me after he checks in on Dakota.

"You right, Knox?" he questions me, following me back into the living area.

I gulp, feeling like a child not a grown man when I say, "Could I talk to you for a moment? In private."

"Sure, everything alright?"

"I hope so," I start, gulping down the lump in my throat. "I was hoping you'd accept me and give me your blessing to ask Dakota to marry me."

Again Mr Neelson is glaring at me, pondering my statement. He rubs the stubble on his chin, murmuring a moment before he matter of factly replies, "After her eighteenth party. Not a moment before."

I nod, but don't reply as he quickly continues, "You seem like a great man Knox...but I'm not exactly happy about you defiling my daughter."

I'm baffled by his words, his assured statement and wonder if he honestly does know I've slept with Dakota. I decide to own up to it. No point denying it.

"I'm sorry, Mr Neelson," I admit, giving him a wary smile. "I know I should've waited until I married her, but I appreciate your permission despite my mistake."

"Of course Knox," he affirms, a smile curving his lips. "I can see my girl loves you. And I'm honestly not surprised of her falling for an older man, and a Vet as well."

That makes me laugh.

"Yeah, she's a natural with animals..." I acknowledge, adding in my head, 'and kids.' Just the thought of that makes me excited. I've always wanted a family of my own, and I can tell from Dakota's interactions with her younger siblings that she'll be an amazing mother.

"Yes, very true," he affirms, and I panic for a moment hoping I didn't say Dakota would be good with kids out loud.

Take My Heart

"Thank you for your blessing Mr Neelson."

"Not a problem, drive safely son," Mr Neelson says as I jiggle my keys in my pocket, signalling I'm ready to leave. I like the sound of that, of Dakota's father calling me son. Like how it sounds sincere and not accusatory like when my father used to say it to me. He leads me out to my car, and getting in I check my phone to find I have a text message from Piper.

K call me.

Starting the engine, once my phone has connected to bluetooth I call Piper. She answers almost straight away.

"Knox, about time brother," she chastises me, her tone frustrated and strained.

"Hey Pipes, what's wrong?" I question my younger sister gripping the steering wheel worriedly.

"Dad threatened me," she declares, her voice monotone. I'm worried, not sure if I should even be driving whilst having this conversation.

"What? How so?"

"The usual...I know something about you Piper Audrie that is unfavourable when your last name is Ellersan," Piper tells me with a mocking tone. "And if your behaviour is not corrected soon, your trust fund is as good as gone."

"Shit Pipes," I answer. "But honestly what the fuck is he talking about?"

"Fucked if I know K. You know he wants me to come and work for him."

I laugh then, replying, "Yeah only because I didn't, Piper."

"Yeah, but I think there's more to it than that," she admits, seeming worried and sounding as though she's cringing. "There's that creepy fucker Jonathan who always hits on me every time he sees me." I nod, even though she can't see me. "And when Dad sees him with me I swear his eyes light up excitedly. It creeps me out."

"Oh god, Pipes!" I bellow, practically screaming the words. "Stay away from him," I warn. "That guy is shadier than dad."

I hate calling Kieran Ellersan dad. He never was worthy of being called dad, too busy with his property empire to be a father.

"I know K. I know," she says with a laugh. "Maybe I should come live with you."

"You're welcome here anytime, Pipes."

"I know K, but my life with my friends and my job is here," she informs me, not very convincingly. "I can't just leave."

"Yeah, anyway Pipes I gotta go," I tell her as I pull up outside the vet clinic. She sighs.

"Ok, K."

"I need to settle the animals for the night," I tell her, turning the engine off but not taking out the key so the bluetooth stays on. "Keep safe, baby sis."

"I will, Knox," she promises, making a kissing sound when she adds, "Kiss the puppies for me."

Take My Heart

I laugh at her cute request.

"Of course, Piper. Love you."

"Love you too, Knox."

Hanging up, I take the key out of the ignition and get out of the car.

Once inside I quickly check all the animals in the clinic for the night, before I head to bed, my mind tumbling with thoughts of how I'm going to propose to Dakota in a couple of weeks after her birthday party.

I want it to be perfect, and a far cry from how I proposed to the bitch I never should've let into my heart. I never should've let Madison take my heart all those years ago. But if I hadn't I'd have never known Dakota, and I can't imagine a future I want more.

I'm right where I should be and Dakota has taken my heart.

It beats for her.

Thirty Nine

Dakota

For weeks Braeden has been acting weird, having hushed conversations with Georgia—when he was over—and with my parents. And I never would've expected those conversations to be about us having a joint eighteenth on the farm.

He's being a dufus, his hands over my eyes as he's hobbling towards the barn with me. With his front to my back it's stupidly awkward, but I can tell he's smiling from the tone in his voice, "Keep going, D. We're not at the barn yet."

"I can't see where I'm going Braeden," I taunt, giddiness in my voice.

"I know that,D, but I won't let anything happen to you," he assures me as we keep shuffling awkwardly forward. "Only a few more metres."

"That means nothing to me," I snap at my brother, causing him to laugh. His hands are suddenly gone from my eyes and I'm in front of the beautiful decorated barn. String lights are hung from the rafters, and hay bales are lined up to form a grand entrance. In the fading light of an early summer evening it looks stunning.

Turning towards my brother, I stretch up onto my tiptoes and envelope him in a hug.

"Thanks for this, you sneaky dufus."

"Anything for you, D," Braeden says with a smile, taking my hand with his.

It's been great getting to know him better these last few months. He's a sweet, caring guy under his tough guy outside persona, and even though he's a month or so younger than me he's become super protective towards me, and I can't say I hate that at all. With my brother and Knox in my corner, I know I'm beyond loved.

"Come on," Braeden says excitedly, "all our friends and significant others are waiting inside for us to get this party started."

Caz May

Following him into the barn, I can see he's right. Practically everyone we know is in our barn, and seeing Braeden and me walk in a hush descends on the space, before a slow clap led by my dad starts to welcome us. Dropping Braeden's hand I hobble up to dad, and hug him.

"Thanks for this, daddy. I love it."

"You're welcome, sweetheart. Enjoy yourself, but don't get drunk now."

I laugh at his serious warning tone. And elbow Braeden in the side to stop him from sniggering beside me.

He whispers in my ear, "You're so getting drunk tonight, huh sis?"

Nodding enthusiastically, I head to the bar on one side of the barn. You'd think it was always there, and that this barn doesn't usually have a menagerie of animals in it.

Sitting down on one of the stools at the bar, I smile at the cute bartender, telling him as calmly as I can, "Make me the dirtiest sounding cocktail you can."

He nods at me, smirking. "One Screaming Orgasm coming right up, birthday girl."

I feel my cheeks heat, hearing the name of the drink, and mutter a 'thanks' sheepishly when the cute bartender presents the drink to me—in a martini glass—with a wink.

Lifting the glass to my lips I take a slow slip, moaning in pleasure as I swallow the sweet, creamy drink down my throat. It's utterly delicious and I completely get the name. I want to scream the roof of the barn off, telling everyone how deliciously good this 'screaming orgasm' is.

Take My Heart

Taking another sip, I know my cheeks are still flushed with all my dirty thoughts, and I nearly spit the drink clear across the bar when I feel someone—my someone—stepping up behind me, and he wraps his arms around my waist. He leans in close, whispering raspy in my ear, "What are you drinking kitten?"

I shift in his arms, tipping my head back so I can look in his eyes when I mutter, "A screaming orgasm, Dr Ellersan."

"Fuck, kitten. I'd love to give you a real screaming orgasm right now," he tells me, desire flashing in his eyes that sends that jolt of pleasure into my knickers.

"This dress does something to a man, kitten," he informs me, grabbing the tight red fabric of my dress.

"You like it?"

"I fucking love it, but I'd love to see it on the floor of my bedroom," he teases with a sexy smirk.

I really love this man. Love that he's not afraid to show he loves me—in public—now. Curse what everyone else thinks, I spin all the way around on the stool, so I'm facing Knox, and I cup his cheeks to pull him down towards me for a kiss. It's a kiss I feel all the way from my lips, to my toes and right into my knickers.

He breaks our lips apart, groaning deeply.

"Damn, kitten. You asking to be fucked right now?"

"Maybe," I tease, smiling at him. "Or we could dance?"

"Anything you want, kitten. If I've got you in my arms right now, I'm happy." Those words make my stomach flip, and explode with butterflies.

Caz May

Getting up off the stool I stumble into Knox's arms, unsteady on the my feet with the moon boot on.

"Careful, kitten," Knox purrs into my ear as he leads me across the dance floor, with his hand in my mine.

Our bodies collide as he pulls me against his body, and we rock together to the slow beat of the music filling the barn.

As we dance I can feel his dick pressing against my belly, and leaning in, up on my tiptoes I whisper against his lips, "Can we get out of here?"

"Not yet kitten, but you're coming home with me tonight." There's promise in his tone, and it makes me giddy.

"Only if you'll give me an actual screaming orgasm," I taunt him, with a peck of a kiss.

"Oh, you bet I will kitten," he promises again, kissing me harder and taking my breath away.

I'm really happy with Knox, he's treating me amazing and I love him with my whole heart.

Forty

Knox

I haven't seen Dakota since the night of her birthday party—both of us busy—me at the clinic and her helping her parents with things at home.

I've missed her, missed having her in my arms. I'm so gone for her I now know I never loved Madison as much as I thought I did, quite possibly at all.

Right now, I'm pacing my apartment, waiting for Dakota to arrive for the night. She's late, and I'm scared that her feelings have changed. That she's found a guy her

Caz May

age, and she doesn't want me anymore. But I don't need to worry, as she's rushing down the hallway of the clinic now with a huge grin.

Reaching me at the door jam, she jumps into my arms and our lips collide in the sweetest of kisses. With her kiss on my lips, I don't doubt her feelings for me a second longer. She loves me as much as I love her.

Breaking the kiss, I whisper, "Hey kitten. Happy to see me?"

"Yes, Knox. I missed you," she coos sweetly, sliding down my body so her feet are back on the tiles. My dick practically groans feeling her body slide over mine.

"Did you lock the front door?"

She giggles.

"Yes, Dr Ellersan. No one is going to interrupt us."

"Music to my ears, kitten," I murmur, grabbing her by the waist and sweeping her into my arms. She peppers kisses all over the stubble on my jawline, and I kick the door closed, before carrying her to the couch.

I barely put her down on the cushions before she's kneeling, and stretching up to kiss me.

Again I break the kiss.

"Slow down kitten, we've got all night."

She pouts, all cute and sexy, and I take a moment to look at her outfit. It's not anything particularly sexy or revealing but it looks so tempting my dick hardens in my shorts.

Take My Heart

"I know, Dr Ellersan, but you look so sexy with the goatee I just want to kiss you."

My mind goes south, and I find myself suggesting, "I think you'd like feeling my stubble somewhere else, kitten."

It's a brazen suggestion, but Dakota's eyes widen and she giggles in her sweet, sexy way.

"Are you going to kiss my pussy?" she asks with innocence in her tone when she utters the word 'pussy' in a dirty way.

"Do you want me too, Dakota?" I ask her, fisting my aching dick in my grip.

"Yes, Dr Ellersan," Dakota purrs. I want to fuck her so much right now, but I also desperately want to feel her come on my tongue again. I've missed everything about her, and it seems like an age since I tasted her.

"Take off these cute little shorts, kitten," I taunt, gripping the waistband of the denim shorts brushing her belly button.

With her eyes locked on mine, she unbuttons them and slips them down her thighs to her knees. She's only wearing skimpy white cotton knickers and damn they're soaked.

"You turned on kitten?"

"Yes, Dr Ellersan," she moans seductively. I'm loving the dirty talk, the way she's calling me doctor Ellersan.

Without another word, I kneel down on the floor, so my face is at her crotch. And I kiss her clit through the fabric. She moans, a loud, "Oh," escaping her lips.

Looking up at her I grip the edge of the knickers, slipping them over her arse, and down her thighs to meet her shorts.

"Spread your legs, kitten," I demand. She shifts her legs apart, stretching the fabric of her knickers and shorts that restrict her movement.

"Knox, please," she begs me, grabbing a fistful of my hair, and shoving my head between her legs. I inhale the scent of her pussy a moment, before kissing her clit and groaning against her body. She starts to buck her hips against my jaw, rubbing her extremely wet pussy over my mouth.

"Oh, shit," she calls out, the curse sounding so illicit from her innocent mouth. "It feels so good."

I stop a moment, looking up at her.

"Come for me, kitten, or I won't fuck you."

My mouth collides with her pussy again, and with a final lick and a kiss against her clit, she comes, thrusting her pelvis against my chin. I lap up every last drop, and stretch up, still on my knees to kiss her. She welcomes the dirty kiss, laving her tongue over my lips and jaw, as she moans and takes the kiss deeper.

With a chuckle I break the kiss.

"You're a dirty girl, kitten."

"You make me want to do all sorts of dirty things, Dr Ellersan," she taunts back, reaching between us to cup my aching dick through my terry shorts.

"Is that so kitten?" I gasp, because her touch feels so good even through the fabric.

"Yeah, do you want to do dirty things to me, Dr Ellersan?" she questions, causing a groan to escape my lips as her hands plunge inside the waistband of my shorts.

"You know I do, Dakota," I taunt her back, not giving a flying fuck that my shorts are now at my knees and I'm naked from the waist down.

"You weren't wearing jocks, Dr Ellersan," Dakota teases, smirking when she adds, "Were you hoping to fuck me?"

I don't reply straight away, instead I stand, and grip her hips to turn her body around so she's facing the back of the couch. Her arse is in the air, and she squeals.

"What're you doing Dr Ellersan?" she questions teasingly, glancing over her shoulder at me as I yank off my t-shirt. She stretches up then, her gaze raking my body as she yanks off her own t-shirt to expose her own nakedness. Her breasts are free—no bra in sight—and her nipples are hard.

"Fuck Dakota, you're so damn beautiful. And sexy as hell."

"You're a work of art, Knox," she replies, trailing her fingers down my abs to my dick.

"Mmm, fuck I need to be inside you Dakota."

"Then fuck me Knox," she jeers, gripping the back of the couch and pushing her pert arse towards me.

"I don't have protection on me right now," I tell her worriedly and inwardly cursing myself for not being better prepared.

She shakes her head, her gaze on my face. And smiling she says, "I don't care. Fuck me and worry about that later."

I want to say something else, say that I don't want to get her pregnant but words like that will ruin this moment, and honestly I want nothing more than to fuck her pussy raw. I'll pull out, I promise to myself as I slide inside her from behind.

She giggles, and mewls, "Feels so good, Dr Ellersan."

It feels better than good. Realising I'm in love with Dakota, and knowing that I'm soon going to ask her to marry me is making the sex unbelievably better.

I still my hips a moment, letting her adjust to the new position before I start thrusting harder. Her moans are loud, and I'm thankful I don't have nearby neighbours who will hear her screaming.

Tentatively I brush my thumb over her arse hole, and she flinches, glaring back at me.

I smile at her. "Trust me kitten," I tell her, pushing my thumb into her unexplored hole. She shifts, pushing back harder on my dick, and gasps before she moans. With my

Take My Heart

other hand I reach down to her clit, and I increase the pace of my thrusts.

"Come for me kitten," I demand, loving how she's controlling the pace of our fuck by meeting my thrusts with her hips.

As though my words are a cue, she starts to tremble, her hips shaking as she comes, calling out, "Knox!" at the top of her lungs.

I pull out, gripping her hips as I come all over her butt and lower back.

"Fuck Dakota," I moan, yanking her up so her back is against my front. I kiss her then, and wrap my arms around her waist.

She breaks the contact of our lips.

"I love you Knox."

"I love you, Dakota," I reply, loving the sweet smile my words cause to show on her face. Standing up I lift her off the couch, and carry her to my bedroom.

She giggles when I drop her on the bed, her gaze watching me shuffle into the bathroom to grab a face washer and condom; just in case she's up for round two.

Back in the room, Dakota squeals when I wipe the face washer over her back and butt to clean her up.

"Better, kitten?" I ask, throwing it aside as I pick her up and put her on the bed properly.

"Yes, Dr Ellersan," she replies, a hint of teasing in her voice which comes out raspy and sexy.

Caz May

Pulling her into my arms I kiss her again, and my dick instantly hardens again. I can't control myself around her. Still kissing, she rocks her pussy against my hardening dick.

"Fuck, kitten, you asking to be fucked again?" I ask, breaking the kiss and staring at her.

"Maybe," she taunts, giggling when I grip her hips.

Kissing her again, I roll us over so she's on top of me straddling my hips. Feeling around on the bed next to me, I grab the condom, ripping the foil open. Dakota shifts back a little, and I roll the condom down over my hard length.

Sitting back against the headboard, I lean in to whisper in Dakota's ear, "I want you to ride me, Dakota. Be my cowgirl."

She smiles and kisses me, impaling herself on my dick. Kissing me harder she starts to bounce up and down on my dick. She can't help but moan, breaking the kiss panting for breath.

"Shit, Knox, shit," she curses, moaning louder as her pace increases.

"Yeah, Dakota, that's my girl," I coerce.

She pants more, moaning even louder, and kisses me again, taking my breath away. She murmurs against my lips, "Knox, I'm going to...it. Feels. So. good," she stammers out between moans, her hips trembling and her pussy clenching around my dick.

Take My Heart

"That's it, kitten. Come for me," I compel, letting go myself and spilling my release into the condom with my hips jerking up.

When we both catch our breath, I brush the stray hairs from her cheeks aside, cupping them as I pull her down to kiss me. My dick softens inside her, and breaking the kiss she slides off, laying down beside me. Discarding the condom—by carelessly yanking it off and throwing it on the floor—I pull Dakota into my arms and cover our naked bodies with the sheets.

"How's your leg, kitten?" I ask her softly, my gaze on her face. "I didn't hurt you did I?"

"No," she says softly. "It's fine. I just like being with you."

I give her a kiss, murmuring after, "I'm glad, kitten. I love being with you as well."

Dakota shifts in my arms, so she's facing me, and cupping my cheeks she kisses me passionately.

"I like being in your space, like here in the apartment but also the vet clinic."

"I like having you here, kitten," I tell her sincerely. My heart falls though when she responds to that with a statement no one wants to hear.

"I've been thinking."

"Oh, um...about what?" I stammer, my heartbeat erratic with my nervousness.

"What I want to do now I've finished school."

Caz May

Sighing in relief I ask, "Any ideas? Are you going to the city?"

She shakes her head.

"I don't want to leave you," she tells me, fighting back tears.

"Aww, kitten, don't cry. I don't want you to leave but don't you want to go to uni?"

"Not if I don't have to. I've actually been thinking about becoming a vet nurse."

I'm sure my eyes light up at her declaration.

"Dakota, that's amazing. You'd be fantastic at it."

"Thanks," she replies, blushing and biting her lip to hold back a question on the tip of her tongue. But I'm sure I know what she's thinking.

"Yes, kitten. You can work here and study online."

"Really? You'd let me do that?"

"Of course. I can't think of anything I want more," I tell her, adding in my head, *'other than having you as my wife.'* I can't wait to ask her to marry me. I have it all planned, and she's going to love it, hopefully.

"Thank you, Knox. I love you," she says, softly kissing me.

I kiss her back, whispering against her lips, "I love you too, Dakota."

We settle in each other's arms then, drifting to sleep, my mind wandering to thoughts of the future together.

Take My Heart

Forty One

Dakota

Sitting on the beanbags in my best friend's bedroom, I can't stop smiling thinking of the last night I spent at Knox's place.

Ava elbows me in the side.

"What's got you smiling like that, Kota?" she questions me, teasingly. "Would it be about a certain hot, older man?"

I feel my cheeks heat with a blush, and looking down at my hands in my lap I mumble, "Might be."

Caz May

"Tell me, Kota. What's happened?"

I wanted to tell Ava literally the next day after I slept with Knox, but I kept quiet, because I'm nervous to talk about anything sexual with my best friend.

I can't look her in the eyes, even when I grab one of her many teddy bears from the floor beside me. Fidgeting with it, I also bite down on my lip.

"Kota, tell me!" Ava squeals, poking me and trying to steal the teddy bear from me. I hold it tighter, against my heart that's beating erratically.

"Fine," I mumble again. "We had sex."

"Ooo, you lost your v-card, girl!"

"Yeah," I reply, blushing again, and looking at my best friend with a smile. "And it got better the second time."

"Definitely does," Ava affirms with a nod. "Did you come?"

"Yeah, more than once," I admit, laughing. "Dr Ellersan knows how to make a girl feel good."

Ava laughs, then replies, "I'm so happy for you, Kota."

"Thanks, A. I'm sorry I didn't tell you sooner."

"That's ok. I get it. Do you love him?"

"Yeah, I love him so much. And he loves me. I'm so happy."

Ava excitedly giggles, and I throw the teddy bear at her head to stop her from laughing.

She catches it, her strong basketball player reflexes kicking in. And she shrieks, "Hey, my Zekey bear gave me that bear."

Take My Heart

"I know. He has a thing for giving you teddy bears."

"Yeah, it's so cute. Always makes me want to jump him when he gives me a new one."

I grab another one, and throw it at her. "You're a dirty girl, A."

She picks up the teddy bears, and throws them back at me.

"You can't talk now, Kota. You're just as dirty now."

I nod because it's true. Knox brings out my dirty girl side.

"That's true," I reply, breaking into a fit of giggles.

Ava laughs as well, asking, "So where have you done it?" She has a cheeky grin on her face.

"Just in my bed, and his bed as well. We got naughty on his couch too."

"Damn Kota. You naughty girl," Ava teases, giggling.

"Yeah, where's the naughtiest place you and Zeke have done it?" I question my best friend, causing her cheeks to colour with a blush.

"In the locker room at school after Grad," she admits, not looking me in the eye.

"Ava! That's so bad!" I shriek.

"Yeah, but damn Kota, it was so hot."

"I bet," I reply, blushing when I add, "I've thought about doing it on one of the treatment tables in the clinic."

"Damn, Kota, that's so dirty," Ava squeals, adding before I can answer, "the cool metal against your butt would be kinda hot."

"Yeah, so dirty," I reply, before breaking into a fit of giggles.

Ava laughs as well. And I'm glad I told her, and opened up to her more. She's honestly the best friend a girl could ask for, and I'm going to miss her so much when she goes to live with Zeke next year. I haven't told her about my plans for next year—that I've made with Knox—because they aren't final yet, and I don't want to jump the gun, just in case things don't go to plan.

Forty Two

Knox

*A*gain I'd barely seen Dakota in the past week with so many appointments in the clinic and her having to look after her younger siblings and the farm again whilst her parents were away.

Thankfully her older sister, Georgia was also staying with her though so she wasn't putting too much stress on her ankle. She was ditching the moon boot this week, which was perfect as her having to wear that all the time was getting annoying I'm sure.

Driving into the farm gates, my nervousness is causing me to grip the steering wheel tightly. Pulling up in front of the farmhouse I honk the horn, causing Toby to bark from his spot in the back of the ute. Dakota rushes out the front door, bounding down from the verandah to my ute. She ruffles the fur of Toby's head and gets into the passenger seat. She's wearing a simple, black t-shirt dress. It hugs her body, and I gulp as my gaze rakes her body.

"Damn, kitten. You look beautiful."

"Thanks, I didn't know where we were going so I went casual."

"It's a surprise," I tell her with a smile as start to drive into the paddocks of the farm.

She's glaring at me, a little annoyed that we're still on her property.

"Knox, where are we going?" she questions me with a huff.

"To where I first fell in love with you, kitten," I tell her smiling, and bouncing on the seat of the ute when we hit a pothole. Dakota lets out a laugh and can't wipe the smile off her face when I stop in the paddock.

As Dakota gets out, I let Toby down from the back of the ute. He's eagerly wagging his tail, and bounds towards Dakota the moment he sees her.

"Toby has something for you, kitten."

Take My Heart

She gives me a perplexed look, laughing as Toby starts running around her legs.

"Check his collar," I instruct her, dropping to my knee when she bends down to check Toby's collar. Finding the engagement ring I've tied on Toby's collar, Dakota shrieks excitedly.

"Oh my gosh, Knox, are you serious?" she asks, pulling the ring off and gazing at me on my knee before her.

"Yes, Dakota. You've taken my heart as yours. Made me believe that I deserve to be loved, and I'd love it if you'd be my wife. Will you marry me kitten?"

"Yes, Dr Ellersan, Knox, yes!" she shrieks again, as I stand and take the ring from her to slip it on her finger. She holds it up to admire and the sunlight catches the single diamond.

Excitedly she stretches up on her tiptoes to kiss me. And Toby excitedly barks at our feet. Grabbing Dakota around the waist I hoist her up onto the tailgate of the ute.

Pushing me down she kisses me, and with the warm sun beating down on us we get lost in kissing each other to celebrate our engagement with Toby running around the paddock showing his excitement as well. Nothing could be more perfect.

Caz May

Forty Three

Dakota

The last few months things have been hectic in my life, with recovery from my accident, looking into Vet nursing and starting wedding planning. We're planning an early January wedding so the pressure is on to get things organised.

Braeden is over for dinner, as he is most Sunday nights since we found out we're half-siblings. Having a brother my own age has been different and I've loved every

Take My Heart

minute of getting to know him more, realising he's not the scary guy he seems with all his tattoos.

After swallowing his bite of roast lamb, he pipes up, "Can't believe you're getting married sis."

I look at my brother with a smile.

"I know, it's crazy," I say, still smiling. "But I'm so happy, with Knox and being able to start work at the clinic soon."

Braeden smiles back.

"Yeah, that's so exciting too. I'm happy for you."

"Thanks, Brae," I reply, gulping down a couple of bites of potato before asking my brother, "Will you be in the wedding party?"

I swear a blush colours his cheeks, which makes me laugh because I don't think much makes my brother blush.

"Yeah, I'd love to, D," he beams at me. "Am I the best man?"

"Maybe. I'll have to check with Knox."

"All good, sis," Braeden replies with a nod, pushing his plate away and standing from his chair.

"I better be getting home," he says to me, then nodding to my parents when he says, "thanks again for dinner, Matilda."

"Anytime, Braeden, dear."

He rounds the table, giving mum a kiss on the cheek, and me a wink before he leaves. I finish up my own dinner, excuse myself, and head to my bedroom to text Knox—my fiancé—about having my brother as our best man. I don't think he'll say no to the request. He's left most of the planning to me, and told me to not worry about the cost of anything. I'm still going to be mindful, but I want a pretty, rustic boho wedding, and I'm wearing cowboy boots under my dress.

My original plan was to go dress shopping with Ava, but when I looked online nothing was striking my fancy. Nothing appeared boho enough. And sitting in the lounge room, I'm gazing around the room at the family photos on the walls.

My parents' wedding photo catches my eye, with my mum in a beautiful floral lace gown. It's exactly what I want, but I have no idea if she even still has it, so many years later.

I can hear her in the kitchen, so closing my laptop I put it down on the coffee table before I head into the kitchen.

"Hi, mum," I say hugging her from behind whilst she's at the sink. "What's for dinner?"

"Just taco's, sweetheart. How're you?"

"I'm good," I reply as mum turns around after I stop hugging her. "But I can't find any wedding dresses I like."

"That's no good, Dakota. Is there something you have in mind?"

"Boho," I say with a smile. "Something lacy like yours was."

Mum's face beams with a wide smile at my mentioning of her dress.

"Do you still have it?"

"Of course. It's in a memory chest in the old barn. Are you asking to wear it?"

"Could I mum? It would mean so much to me."

She reaches out to hug me.

"I would love that, Dakota. I'll get dad to get it out so you can try it on tomorrow."

"Thank you, mum," I reply, kissing her cheek. "I'm going to invite Ava, and Ariel over as well if that's ok?"

"Of course, dear," she affirms before asking, "Can you get your brother and sister to wash up for dinner?"

"No worries," I reply, already heading down the hallway to Nebraska and Montana's rooms. I'm feeling excited about seeing mum's dress. I really hope it's the dress of my dreams.

The next day Ava, and Ariel are sitting on my bed as mum wheels the old chest into my room.

"Are you ready?" she asks me, bending down in front of the chest.

I'm on edge, waiting on bated breath as mum flips open the latches. The lid flies up, and reaching inside she pulls out the most beautiful lace, floral motif wedding dress. It has a slight train that flares out, and spaghetti

Caz May

straps with a criss-cross detail over the back. It's absolutely stunning and I can't help but let out a little squeal of delight.

I pull my t-shirt dress over my head, not caring that I'm only in skimpy underwear with my friends in the room. It's not like me, but I'm too damn excited to care. And we're all girls here.

Mum holds it out, the zip lowered and I step into it. Slipping the straps up my arms I turn around and mum zips me up, her hands on my hips as I turn around to face my friends and her, grinning from ear to ear.

"Oh my, Dakota, my dear," Mum gasps. "It fits you perfectly."

Ava squeals, shrieking, "Kota, you look so pretty!"

I turn to the mirror to admire myself, and a tear comes to my eyes. I look and feel so grown up. And I can't wipe the smile off my face.

"It suits you, Dakota," Ariel says. "It's so exciting that you're getting married."

I turn back towards my friends and smile at them both. "I know, and I'm so excited to have you guys in my wedding party. I'm sorry you can't be partnered with Brae though, Ar's."

"That's ok. He's so excited to be the best man for you and Knox."

"Yeah, and who knows it might be you guys getting married next," I say with a laugh.

Take My Heart

"I don't know about that," Ariel replies, blushing, and looking towards mum.

"Well, Dakota dear, let's put the dress away until the big day."

I nod and mum undoes the zip, helping me out of the dress, putting it back in the chest before she leaves my room after giving me a quick hug.

I slip my dress back on, and sit on my desk chair, swivelling the wheels to scoot closer to the bed.

Ariel is almost in tears, and I'm afraid I've said something to upset her. That something bad has happened between her and Brae, or Briston.

"Ar's, are you ok?"

"Yeah, I'm fine. I'm just happy for you."

Ava puts a hand on her thigh, smiling at her, and asking the question I was thinking, "Has something bad happened with you and Brae? Or Bris?"

"No, nothing like that. I...I um...just think we're kinda drifting apart."

Ava and I both gasp at her words.

"What do you mean? You guys are goals, Ar's," Ava says her voice high pitched.

"I mean, I love them both...but Bris has been a bit closed off lately. And I feel like as a threesome we're drifting apart unless we're fucking."

"So you think Bris doesn't love you anymore?"

"I don't know. I think he loves Braeden more, but it's complicated."

Caz May

"Sounds like it," I say softly, then asking curiously, "Do you love one of them more?"

Ariel nods, replying with a hiccuping sob, "Yeah, I hate to admit it, but I love Braeden more. I've always loved Briston and I always will, but Braeden has a bigger piece of my heart."

Ava replies, "Makes sense, Ar's. Braeden loves you more as well, I know it."

"Has he said something to you?" Ariel asks Ava.

"Not in so many words, but I could tell when he was confused about his sexuality. He's been in love with you long before he loved Briston."

"Yeah, I loved Briston before I loved Braeden, but I have a deeper connection with Braeden."

Ava smiles and then laughs. "Admit it, Ariel, the sex with Braeden is better, huh?"

Ariel smiles then, blushing with her reply, "Yeah, sex with Braeden is off the charts amazing. With Briston, it's sweet and caring."

"Best of both worlds," Ava replies. "Pity you can't marry them both."

"Yeah, damn shame," Ariel replies. "But honestly I'm not thinking about that happening yet. After uni maybe."

"Yeah, same," Ava replies. "But honestly, I'd marry Zeke tomorrow if he asked me today."

Ariel and I both nod at her and break into giggles.

Take My Heart

"Who are we?" I question them, still laughing when I add, "Talking about marriage, and me actually getting married."

"We're growing up, Kota. Becoming women," Ava says, and again all three of us start giggling.

I'm so damn lucky to have such amazing friends, and even luckier to be marrying the most amazing man in a month's time. Growing up is scary, but exciting.

Forty Four

Knox

Quite possibly it's stupid I'm nervous about calling my younger sister. I guess I'm scared she's going to tell me I'm an idiot to be marrying a girl that's even younger than her.

But Piper has never been judgemental and has always told me like it is...not that I listened to my wise beyond her years little sister. If I had I'd have dodged the bullet of the heartbreak with Madison, but then I also never would've moved to Lockgrove Bay, and I'd have never met Dakota. And let my beautiful girl take my heart as hers.

Plonking down on the couch, I sigh as I dial Piper's number, hoping that maybe she won't answer, but also hoping that she does.

"Hey, K. What's up big brother?" she answers with her chipper tone that makes me feel at ease.

"Hey Pipes, I need to tell you something."

She exhales a loud breath, as though she's worried about what I'm about to say.

"It's not bad, Piper. I'm not dying or anything like that."

"Well, you never know," she says with a laugh, before questioning me, "So why are you calling then, K?"

"I'm getting married, and I'd love for you to be in the wedding."

"Seriously, K!" she shrieks down the phone and I'm worried she's about to jump through the receiver and strangle me.

"Yeah, I'm happy Pipes. Dakota is such a sweet girl, and perfect for me."

"Girl?" Piper questions, the tone in her voice intrigued and worried.

"Yeah, girl, Piper. Dakota is eighteen, but very mature for her age."

"Well, I'm surprised but you deserve to be happy, K."

"I am happy, Pipes."

"Good, big bro, and yes I'd love to be in your wedding."

"Great, Dakota's younger brother is the best man and her best friend is the maid of honour," I tell my sister, hoping she's not offended by not being the maid of honour. "I'm not sure who you'll be partnered up with yet."

She laugh softly and then sweetly says, "That's okay big brother. I'm just happy to be in your wedding."

I respond with a laugh as well.

"Thanks Pipes. I love you little sis."

"So, K, when is the big day?"

"It's a week from today. I should've told you sooner but I was scared."

"You're a dufus, Knox José Ellersan."

"Is that too short notice Pipes?"

Piper again laughs at my question.

"No Knox, it's not. I could do with a chance to get away. Where are you living now anyway?"

"Lockgrove Bay," I declare with happiness.

"Okay big brother. I will head to you on Thursday," Piper tells me, matching my tone.

"Sounds great Piper. I will see you when you get here."

"No worries, Knox. I'm really excited," she tells me before her voice drops low, "have you told the parentals?"

"No, and don't you go blabbering it to dad either. I don't want him there."

I cringe saying 'dad'. I hate calling my father that, as he doesn't deserve the title of being called that. And I'm a hundred percent serious that I don't want him at my wedding this time.

"I won't tell daddy not so dear but what about Mum? She'll be an emotional wreck if she's not there K."

"I'll tell her, straight after I get off the phone with you. And yes, you can bring her with you."

"Good, you'd regret it if she wasn't K."

"I know, Pipes," I admit with a sigh. "See you both on Thursday."

"Bye, K. Kiss the puppies for me," she tells me, blowing kisses into the phone. I don't get to reply before my little sister hangs up and I go to dial my mum to tell her my news.

Part of me doesn't want either of my parents at my wedding, but Mum had always tried to be supportive and stick up for me against Kieran Ellersan. She was blinded by her love for him, but she also loved Piper and me fiercely, and maybe her coming to Lockgrove Bay might finally open her eyes as well.

I'm just closing up the clinic, saying goodbye to the final patient of the day—and for the next few days with my wedding happening—when the door swings open again with Piper and my mother arriving.

"Hello, Dr Ellersan," Piper sasses rushing up to me to hug me.

Hugging her tightly I glance over her shoulder to mum who seems like she wants to say something, but she's holding back. Her eyes are on mine, but also scanning the reception area of the clinic when I pull away from Piper's hug.

My sister seems a bit scattered, not herself. I shrug that thought away for a moment, looking at mum when I greet her warmly, "Hi Mum, it's lovely to see you."

She smiles then, but it's tentative, hiding her fear.

"Thank you, Knox darling. I'm delighted you invited me," she says, her voice monotone. It sends panic through me, worry that the door is going to swing open again to reveal an intruder, an wanted guest. Mum must be able to sense my hesitation.

"He's not here, Knox." Her face falls, and Piper pulls her against her side in comfort. The gesture has me worried for my mum and younger sister but I don't push the issue. Piper's glare is enough to warn me from asking any questions, and tells me she won't tell me what's wrong.

"Well, let's get you both settled," I state, stepping behind them to lock the front door.

They follow me down the hallway into the apartment, dragging their suitcases behind them to the guest room.

"It's lovely Knox," Mum informs me, running a hand over the velvet comforter. "Do you mind if I have a lie down?"

Take My Heart

"Of course, Mum. We'll be in the kitchen if you need us," I tell mum, as Piper follows me out of the room.

In the kitchen I start making coffee's, and Piper sits on the breakfast bar stool sighing deeply.

"Is everything ok, Pipes?"

"Yes Knox. Don't worry about anything."

"Don't give me that crap, Piper Audrie. Something is up with mum and you for that matter."

"Now is not the time to tell you," she states, taking the coffee I hand to her and slowly sipping it.

"It's your special event, your wedding K."

"Yes Piper it is, but you're my little sister and I care about you."

"It's fine Knox ok. You just need to enjoy your wedding, and appreciate the fact that mum is even here." I don't like her tone. There is definitely something she's not telling me, which isn't helping my nerves at all.

"I'm jittery after last time," I admit, taking a gulp of my coffee.

Piper chuckles softly.

"Don't be, K. Madison wasn't the right woman for you."

"Yeah, I know. Still the thought of a wedding makes me nervous."

"Well, is this wedding in a church with gigantic wooden doors?"

"No, it's outside on Dakota's farm, so a far cry from a church."

Caz May

"Then stop overthinking. Because you know what I think, Knox José Ellersan?" my little sister says in a teasing tone.

"What do you think Piper Audrie Ellersan?" I tease back with a smile.

"Dakota seems like the perfect woman for you. An animal lover just like you."

"Yeah, Pipes," I reply with a wide smile, thinking of my Dakota as I take the final sip of my coffee. "I think you might be right about that. A love of animals is a special connection we have, and I honestly love her with my whole heart."

Piper returns the smile.

"I'm glad Knox. You deserve so much happiness big brother." She gets off the stool then, and asks, "Do you mind if I have a shower? Need to wash off the city and travel grime."

"Of course, bathroom is the door over there. Towels and stuff is in there."

"Thanks, K," she replies, heading to the bathroom.

I just nod, turning my attention to the discarded coffee cup she left most of.

Something is definitely up, something that I feel is going to break my heart. But now is not the time to probe my sister about it.

This weekend is going to be full of happiness—not heartbreak like the last time I attempted to get married.

Take My Heart

I'd made a mistake letting myself fall for Madison. But this time around, I'm sure falling for Dakota is no mistake.

Forty Five

Dakota

Glancing around the restaurant it's blurry and I can't focus.

I'm drunk, having had too many strawberry daiquiris. I suck in the last sips of the one in front of me—through the Penis straw—poking out of it. The last sips make a slurping, gurgling sound and I giggle, spitting it across the table, straight into Chastity's hair. She shrieks, "Eww, Dakota. You spat in my hair!"

Take My Heart

In a blur, she stands, her chair grating on the floor. Ava glares at her with an angry expression.

"Chas, where are you going?" my best friend asks.

"I'm leaving, A-va. I shouldn't have even come to this party."

Ava laughs. "Well, we aren't stopping you, Chastity. Kota just wanted to be nice when she invited you, but sadly you can't be a decent human and be nice back."

Chastity huffs, scooping up her handbag from the floor and stumbling out on her high heels.

Ava looks at me then. She's a bit blurry, and I rub my eyes to focus on her.

"Why did you invite her Kota?"

"Cause…I…I…not a…b…b…itch," I stutter.

"She's the bitch, Dakota," Ariel says from across the table.

"Yeah, she prob…ab…ly…w…ou…ld've try to fuck Kn… ox," I stammer again, practically incoherently because I'm so drunk.

"Wouldn't have put that past her," Ava replies. "She's been with two of our guys in the past, and tried to get it on with Zeke twice."

"She seems like a ho, Dakota. Did you invite her to the wedding?" my new soon-to-be sister-in-law Piper asks me.

"No, thank goodness," I reply, hiccuping and then burping loudly. It causes the girls to laugh, and Ariel says, "Do you always hiccup and burp after sucking on appendages, Kota?"

Confused I huff, "What do you mean, Ar's?"

They all laugh again.

"She means when you suck Knox's dick, Kota," Ava informs me.

"Eww, Ava. I don't need to think about my new little sister sucking my brother's dick," Piper says, gagging.

"Sorry," Ava replies, taking a sip of her own daiquiri, through a penis straw.

I have to admit something to my friends.

"I haven't done that," I confess, hiccuping again.

Ava and Ariel gape at me, and Piper sighs in relief.

"Seriously, Kota? You haven't sucked his dick?" Ava questions, her voice really high pitched.

"No, I don't know how to," I admit, my voice a lot less shaky than before, even though my head is still spinning from too many daiquiri's.

"Kota, Kota, Kota," my best friend singsongs, pushing her half-drunk daiquiri across the table towards me.

"I don't need more drink, A," I tell her.

Ariel and Piper both laugh, and Ariel winks at Ava. They're planning something dirty.

"You're going to practice," Ava tells me with a giggle.

Piper gags.

"I'm going to the bathroom. I can't watch this."

I'm about to tell her that I'm coming with her, almost out of my chair when Ava pulls me back down.

"Sit, missy, and suck on that straw, like you want to suck on Knox's dick."

Again I huff, but put the straw in my mouth, sucking in the cool liquid.

"Woah, Kota, slow down girl," Ariel warns.

"Yeah, Kota, go slow, and swirl your tongue around the tip," Ava tells me, laughing when Ariel smiles at her.

Removing the straw from my mouth, I swallow down the daiquiri in my mouth.

"You're meanies," I spit at them.

"No, but you're a pro," Ava teases.

"Yeah, I'm going to do it," I declare. "Now, tonight."

"Your man isn't here, Kota," Ariel states.

"I know, but I can go home with Piper," I say, nodding towards the bathroom where she's now coming back from.

I jump out of my chair, stumbling towards my new sister.

"We're leaving," I tell her.

"Oh, um, ok," she stammers, looking towards my friends.

Ava laughs and says to Piper as she grabs her bag, "I hope you've got earplugs, Piper."

Piper laughs back.

"If only."

Ava and Ariel stand, and I pull them into a hug.

"Love you, my besties. I'm going to go give my man a dick suck."

Piper scoffs behind me, ushering me out of the restaurant. Glancing back I see her roll her eyes at my

Caz May

giggling best friends. I'm giddy—still drunk—but I'm going to suck Knox's dick until he's having a screaming orgasm.

Stumbling inside the clinic I'm miaowing like a kitten. Piper is walking behind me and she's laughing at me.

"Dakota, are you alright?"

"Knox calls me 'kitten'," I tell her, pushing the door of his apartment open.

"Um, ok, well I'm going to bed," Piper says, brushing past me.

"Ok," I say softly before calling out, "Doctor Ellersan! Are you here?"

No reply comes, so stumbling towards his room I try to hold in my giddy laughter.

I'm going to suck Dr Ellersan's dick.

It's so dirty.

My lips—my mouth—is going to be on his dick, and I'm going to suck on it like I did on the penis straws, and lick it like a lollipop.

Licking my lips in anticipation I fumble with handle of his bedroom door, getting frustrated that it doesn't want to turn to let me in.

But thankfully it eventually cooperates and the door opens.

Giggling I sneak in, dropping to my knees I crawl across the floor like a kitty cat. His bed has the covers pulled back but he's not in it. My heart sinks for a moment, until I get closer to the ensuite and hear water shut off.

Take My Heart

Continuing to crawl across the floor towards the ensuite I miaow, trying to sound like I'm miaowing 'Dr Ellersan'. And when I get to the ensuite door I bump into his legs—his grey trackie pant legs—as he turns to leave the bathroom.

"Dakota!" he shrieks in surprise as I glare up at him, licking my lips. "What're you doing here? And crawling across my bedroom floor?"

"I'm a kitten," I mewl at him.

"You're drunk Dakota."

"So, Dr Ellersan," I stutter, annoyed. He tries to walk out of the bathroom, but I grab his ankles. He's angry with me. And scowling. He looks sexy.

"Get up off the floor, Dakota," he demands, still scowling. It's not fair he can look so sexy all the time.

"No!" I respond, stretching up, but still kneeling so I can reach his waistband. Grabbing it, I laugh as I dak him.

"Dakota, seriously what are you doing?" he questions me, still with the annoyed—angry—scowl.

His dick is there, right in my face, and not hard, but it's long, like one of those lollipops, or Dagwood dogs you get at the fair.

"This," I tell him, grabbing his dick and putting it in my mouth. I gag on it, because it's on my tongue and it tastes funky.

Knox groans, which I think is good, but I don't know. I've never been good at sucking on things. I accidentally suck up bubble detergent instead of blowing bubbles, I'm such a dufus.

"Fuck, Dakota," Knox curses, and then says loudly, "Stop, please, kitten."

With my lips still wrapped around his dick, I glance up at him, and ask through my teeth, "Why? Is it not good?"

When he screeches, "No! Ouch! No!" at the top of his lungs as my teeth sink into his flesh I know I've made a mistake. I failed at giving him a blowjob.

Tears start dripping down my cheeks, and I pull back, collapsing in a heap on his floor crying.

"Dakota, please sweetheart, don't cry," Knox soothes, bending down next to me.

Glancing up at him, I see he's pulled up his trackies, and he's crouching on the floor.

"I hurt you," I stammer. "I bit your dick."

"It's fine, Dakota. I'll live," he teases.

"Not funny, Dr Ellersan," I reply back, sitting up and slapping his arm. "I guess you don't want to marry me now."

"Why wouldn't I want to marry you anymore, kitten?"

"Cause I can't even give you a blowjob."

He laughs, and pulls me into his arms, picking me up effortlessly, and without a word. Melting into his arms, I groan when he puts me down on the bed. He kneels on the edge, leaning down to give me a soft, sweet kiss.

"Practice makes perfect, kitten, and we have the rest of our lives to practice."

Take My Heart

"I guess so," I reply, cupping his stubbled jaw to bring his lips back down to mine for another kiss. He moans against my lips, falling against me as he deepens it.

Breaking the kiss, he shifts to slide into the bed with me, and pulls up the covers over us.

Kissing my forehead he murmurs, "I love you, Dakota. Get some sleep now, kitten."

Shifting in his arms that are over my stomach I softly reply, "I love you too, Dr Ellersan."

I'm sure he replies, but I'm already drifting to sleep.

Forty Six

Knox

1 can't believe I'm standing under a wedding arch, about to marry Dakota. Her brother Braeden is standing by my side as the best man, and next to him as groomsmen is my closest childhood friend Cameron and my friend from uni Bruce. I'd wanted one of them as my best man, but when Dakota asked if Braeden could be the best man I couldn't resist giving into her, with the sweet puppy dog eyed look she gave me.

Take My Heart

Braeden smiles at me as the music starts to swell, signalling the girls arrival.

"Are you ok, Knox?" he asks me, his gaze on my hands I'm anxiously rubbing together.

"Yeah, Braeden. Just can't wait to see her, and hoping like hell she makes it down the aisle," I reply with a snigger to hide the nervousness from my voice.

"She will," he assures me, adding with a squeeze of my arm, "My sister loves you."

I don't get to reply, as his gaze turns to the end of the aisle with the first of the girls walking in to the strong instrumental music.

It's his girlfriend Ariel as one of the bridesmaid's, and the love he feels for her is written all over his face. She looks stunning in the halter neck, floor length blush pink gown. Her dark hair is up from her face in a bun, and her smile is wide as she looks to Braeden, her steps steady down the cowhide aisle that's set up in the paddock of Dakota's family farm, right where I proposed to her a few months ago.

When Ariel reaches the front of the aisle, she gives me a kiss on the cheek with a sweet smile, before she gives Braeden a kiss on the lips and goes to stand on the opposite side of the arch. He can't stop staring at her, even when Piper starts coming down the aisle, slightly quicker than Ariel did.

When she reaches me, her smile is wide, and I hug her. She whispers in my ear, "She looks stunning, big brother."

Caz May

"I don't doubt that, Pipes."

My sister goes to stand on the opposite side of the aisle, and Ava starts the walk down the aisle.

Only a few minutes have passed, but it feels like hours. All I want is to see Dakota heading down the aisle, to be under the arch with me and making a commitment to me. It's a deja vu feeling, and I rock on my heels to try and tamp down my nervousness. Ava gives me a smile that I return, before my gaze is back on the end of the aisle.

This is it.

Dakota is standing at the end of the aisle, her arm linked with her dad's.

Her simple lace dress dips low in the front, fitting her sweet curves perfectly, and her long blonde hair is slightly curled and flowing free over shoulders. To say she looks stunning would be an understatement. My Dakota is completely breathtaking.

The music changes to 'Amazed' by Lonestar, and my girl is heading down the aisle towards me.

Tears sting my eyes, and I swipe my white dress shirt sleeve across my cheeks, sniffing them back. I can't help but smile, so wide my face feels like it's going to crack.

Reaching the end of the cowhide aisle, her dad kisses her on the cheek and I step forward to meet her under the arch. She hands Ava her bouquet of white roses and green eucalypts leaves, wrapped in twine and she takes my hands with hers, ready to take our vows.

Take My Heart

I nod to the celebrant who smiles and begins,"Welcome, loved ones. Thank you all for coming today to share in this wonderful occasion. Today we are here together to unite Knox Jose' Ellersan and Dakota Abigail Neelson in marriage."

The celebrant pauses, looking out to our family and friends on the white fold up chairs.

"Is there anyone here present today, who objects to this union?" the celebrant questions, and I take a breath in, holding it expectantly. I'm envisioning my father careening down the aisle screaming.

But it doesn't happen and the celebrant continues.

"Well, with that out of the way, let's get on with things."

She nods towards me, and I take Dakota's hands with mine as she asks, "Do you Knox, take Dakota to be your lawfully wedded wife, to live together in marriage, to love her, comfort her, honour and keep her, in sickness and in health, in sorrow and in joy, to have and to hold, from this day forward, as long as you both shall live?"

My smile is wide when I reply, "I do." Dakota is grinning so wide as well.

"Do you Dakota, take Knox to be your lawfully wedded husband, to live together in marriage, to love him, comfort him, honour and keep him, in sickness and in health, in sorrow and in joy, to have and to hold, from this day forward, as long as you both shall live?"

Caz May

She giggles sweetly replying with an eager nod, "Yes, I do."

The celebrant smiles, looking out to our family and friends.

"Knox and Dakota have also chosen to express their own vows to each other and have chosen rings to exchange with each other as a symbol of their unending love."

My heart is hammering in my chest, and I'm finding it hard to breathe. I'm about to tell Dakota how much I love her, how much she means to me.

"Dakota, I love you, absolutely adore you. You have brought me back to life. And I can't thank you enough for taking me into your heart. I promise to walk by your side forever and to love, help, and encourage you in all that you want to do. I will take the time to talk to you, to listen to you and to care for you. Through all the changes in our lives, good and bad I will always be there for you, as your strength and comfort. All that I am and all that I have is yours, now and forevermore. This is my promise to you."

She's smiling so wide, her eyes welling with tears. The crowd of our friends is swooning over my words.

"Dakota, your vows for Knox?" the celebrant prompts.

"Knox, I love you, completely and with all my heart. You helped me become a woman, and I'm so beyond happy that you've taken my heart. I promise to help you live your dreams, and accept all of you. I will always listen to you, and accept your love and care in all that happens

Take My Heart

to us. I know that with you by my side I'm loved, and I'm yours forever."

I'm the one crying now. Her words were simple, but mean so much. I just want to kiss her, take her away from here and make love to her—as my wife—all night but there's still formalities of the ceremony and night to come.

"Knox and Dakota will now exchange rings," the celebrant announces, nodding to Braeden who plucks out a tiny pillow out of his pocket with two simple gold rings tied to it.

Taking it, and sliding the ring onto Dakota's finger I say the words we'd practiced the day before, "I give you this ring. Wear it to remind you of the love I have for you on this day and forevermore."

Dakota takes the other ring, and slips it onto my finger, sniffing back tears when she repeats the words, "I give you this ring, Knox. Wear it to remind you of the love I have for you on this day and forevermore."

The celebrant lets out a delighted squeal.

"By the authority vested in me by the state of Victoria, I now pronounce you husband and wife! You may kiss the bride!"

And I don't hesitate to do just that, snaking an arm around Dakota's waist and drawing her into my arms and kissing her passionately.

Cheers and clapping erupts around us, and breaking the kiss we start to walk down the aisle, holding hands.

Our family and friends congratulate as with hugs, and cheek kisses.

It's definitely the happiest day of my life thus far.

Take My Heart

Forty Seven

Dakota

The whole day has been a whirlwind, an amazing one and I'm completely knackered but eager for my first night with Knox as my husband.

Ava had caught the bouquet and Zeke swept her into his arms and kissed her. I'd thought he was going to fall to his knees and propose to her that very moment, but he didn't and my best friends heart broke a little. I could see it in her eyes.

Caz May

Knox—my husband—is driving us to the bed and breakfast in Lorne where we're going to spend our first official night together.

Soft music is playing through the speakers of Knox's Mercedes, but he isn't saying a word. His silence is unnerving, giving me a sense of worry that he's regretting marrying me.

"Are you ok, Knox?" I ask meekly breaking the silence.

"Yeah, perfect kitten," he replies, glancing across at me for a moment as he navigates the windy road. "Just concentrating on the road, is all."

"Oh, are we nearly there?"

"Yeah, kitten, you antsy?"

I giggle softly. "I'm only wearing a g-string, and it's soaked thinking about being with you, Dr Ellersan."

"Is it now, kitten?" he taunts, not really as a question but more a statement. He presses harder on the accelerator, pushing the car forward a little faster but still handling it expertly.

"Yes, and you're a good driver husband."

His breath hitches hearing my words, my calling him husband. And he nods his thanks, startling me when he turns off down a secluded road.

My face must show my horror, as he laughs and says, "Don't worry kitten. I'm not taking you somewhere to off you."

I sigh and laugh.

Take My Heart

"Good to know, but this place is definitely in the middle of nowhere."

Again Knox nods, pulling into a carpark out the front of a beautiful cottage. He cuts the engine and is out of the car before I can even think to move.

Opening the car door, he extends a hand to me and helps me to my feet. And giggling I hitch up the hem of my dress—showing off my cowgirl boots—as I race up onto the verandah.

"What're you waiting for husband?" I call out to Knox who's still standing by the car, dumbfounded.

Closing the car door he runs up behind me, grabbing me around the waist and hauling me into his arms, full bridal style.

Craning my neck to kiss him, my heart rate accelerates when he kicks open the wooden door of the cottage open, and he stalks towards the bedroom.

Lowering me to the bed, he leans over to kiss me again.

"I love you, Dakota, my beautiful wife," he whispers between kisses that continue down my neck and to my cleavage.

"I love you too, Knox, my gorgeous husband," I reply, gasping when his lips brush against my nipple through the lace of my dress.

He looks up at me expectantly. "Are you not wearing a bra, kitten?"

I shake my head, sitting up to slide the straps over my shoulders. The dress drops from my breasts and Knox groans appreciatively.

"Fuck, wife," he taunts, smirking at me when he palms my breast in his hand. "You're so fucking stunning. Your body makes a man weak."

That sounds hot but strikes me as odd. "Oh, not hard?" I question, gazing at him as he stands his full height, and starts to strip from his dress shirt. I watch him undress, each item of clothing falling to the floor torturously slow until he's fully naked and most definitely hard.

"Definitely hard Dakota. But a man could, and I will fall to my knees for you. That's how you make me weak."

"Oh," I stammer, short on words for how those words make me feel, even after today when he's declared his vows to me.

"Dakota, you need to get that pretty dress off," he demands, falling against me, his arms snaking around my back to the zipper.

"And if I keep it on?" I taunt him, my eyes directly on his.

"Then I won't make love to you until the sun comes up."

I don't reply, instead, I inhale a hushed breath as he slides the zipper down, and lightly pushes me down on the bed, so he can pull the dress off over my hips.

When it hits the floor I go to remove my boots, but Knox laughs, smirking like a sexy beast when he requests,

Take My Heart

"Leave those on and wrap those sexy legs of yours around my arse whilst I make love to you, kitten."

I only nod, as he steps in between my legs, leaning over to kiss me as he slides inside my body, making us one again.

Still with him seated inside me, I do as he requested wrapping my legs around his butt to pull him closer, taking him in deeper. His thrusts are slow, steady, and each time he rocks in and out he pushes deeper inside me. It's euphoric, and has my heart hammering in my chest.

He kisses me again, whispering against my lips, "I love you Dakota, my wife."

"I love you, too, Knox, my husband," I affirm back, rocking my pelvis up to meet his, my legs tightening around his butt to pull him deeper than ever.

He groans, stopping his thrusts a moment.

"Damn, kitten. You're going to make me come if you keep doing that."

I laugh, ignoring his request to not buck my hips towards his.

"Is that so Dr Ellersan?" I taunt, smiling at him.

"Yes, kitten," he growls, reaching between us to thumb my clit.

"Knox!" I scream out, that touch and his hard deep thrust sending me careening over the edge. I'm trembling with the most explosive orgasm, and Knox follows, spilling his release inside me as he calls out, "Dakota! I love you!"

He collapses on my chest, pressing a kiss to my forehead.

We're still for a moment, coming down from our high. He shifts, pulling out of my body and standing.

Grabbing my hands he pulls me to my feet, into his arms. He doesn't say a word, leading me into the bathroom that has a massive spa bath in the corner.

Dropping my hand he turns the water on, letting it fill as he pours in some creamy bubble bath.

As we wait for it to fill, he pulls me into his arms, and kisses me, passionately and all-consuming.

"Forever, Dakota Abigail Ellersan," he whispers to me, sending my heart soaring.

"Forever, Knox José Ellersan," I reply back, kissing him again before he shuts off the water and we climb into the warm water together, holding each other tightly, my back to his front.

Our night is just beginning and so is our forever together.

Take My Heart

Forty Eight

Dakota

Standing outside the vet clinic, I'm bouncing up on the balls of my feet, cursing that the concrete is hot as blazers.

My best friend is standing next to me, a blubbering mess.

"Kota, I'm going to miss you so much."

"I'm going to miss you too, A, but you're going to be living with your man," I say through my sobs. "And trust me that's so awesome."

"I honestly can't believe you're married, Kota," she says, smiling at me, "and that I caught the bouquet."

"Yeah, so crazy. Can't wait for you to get married to Zeke."

My best friend sniffs back a sob, her eyes on the footpath.

"I don't know if that will happen anytime soon."

"It will Ava. You're moving in with him, and he loves you so much."

She smiles then says giddily, "It's up to Zeke. But I think it will happen soon."

"I hope so A," I admit, feeling her sadness.

Again she sniffs and then laughs.

"I can't believe we're talking about marriage. What's next? Babies?"

"Oh god, I don't even want to think about that," I reply, shaking my head to stop the memories of changing my siblings' nappies flooding my head.

"Yeah me either, but I really hope Zeke asks me to marry him soon."

"He will, and it will be super cute, probably with a teddy bear," I say laughing.

"Yeah, my Zekey bear loves giving me teddy bears. I have quite the collection."

"Yeah, are you taking them all with you?" I question her, nodding towards her car parked on the street.

She shakes her head, replying, "Nah, only the first one he gave me for my sixteenth birthday.

"Oh," I stammer, wondering why she only wants that one.

"It's my fave because he gave it to me before we first kissed," she tells me smiling wide.

"That's so corny, but super sweet A."

She laughs sweetly, and I pull her into a hug, squeezing her tightly.

"Do you have to go A?"

"Yeah, Kota. I want to have a few weeks to settle in before uni starts," she informs me, not able to hide her smirk.

"A few weeks fucking Zeke twenty-four seven, huh?"

She blushes, and we both laugh.

"Yeah, you got me, bestie. And honestly when did you get so dirty?"

"When I fell in love with Knox. He's a dirty man."

"I bet. I love that you've found someone so great, Kota."

I nod and hug her again, this time sniffing back tears. She pulls back from the hug, and gets her keys out of her pocket, swinging them around on her finger.

"I really gotta get going Kota," she tells me, backing away towards her car. "But I'll let you know when I get there."

"Ok, I love you Ava. Don't forget about me."

"Never, Dakota," she singsongs, opening her car door, and adding, "And I love you too bestie forever."

She gets in the car, starting the engine and reversing out onto the main street. She honks her horn, waving at me in the rearview mirror.

I'm so proud of her, and I know she's proud of me too.

I'm super excited to be starting my apprenticeship in Veterinary nursing with my husband by my side in a few weeks time as well. I'd never dreamed my life was going to turn out so amazing and heading inside my new home—the vet clinic—I can't wipe the smile from my face, especially when I head into the apartment to find Knox coming out of the shower looking deliciously sexy with water droplets running down his abs.

I saunter up to him—and kiss him—pushing the towel from around his waist to the floor.

"Is Ava gone?" he asks, breaking the kiss.

"Yeah," reply solemnly. "I'm going to miss her."

"I bet. Are you sure you're happy with me, staying here?"

"Yes, Knox Ellersan," I say, kissing him again. "I'm beyond happy that I let you take my heart. There's nowhere else I'd rather be than by your side."

"Then I'm happy too, Dakota. I love you, my kitten."

"I love you too, Dr Ellersan," I reply, kissing him again.

He breaks the kiss, grabbing me around the waist and picking me up to take me into our bedroom.

Take My Heart

Being with him is far beyond anything I could've imagined. I'm beyond glad I waited for him, my perfect man who is the only one for me.

Our love of animals brought us together, and even though I said I wasn't ready for babies to Ava the thought of filling our home with animals and babies is at the forefront of my mind.

I want all that and more—forever—with Knox Ellersan, the man who took my heart.

Epilogue

Dakota

It feels surreal that I'm standing in the vet clinic, working there with Knox by my side. We're getting ready for the day, with our first patient about to come in and I pull out my phone from my pocket to text Braeden to see if he settled in ok at uni.

Hey brother

What's up sis?

You settle in ok?

Take My Heart

Yeah sweet digs. Rooming with bris and some other dude who has a stick up his arse.

Eww, Brae. I don't need to hear that especially when I'm about to stick a thermometer up a dogs butt.

Sorry D, I'll let you get back to your swish new job. Say hello to your hubby from me.

Of course, say hi to Bris and Ar's. And send me some pics or get ya butt on insta.

Ok muah muah love ya sis

Love ya back Brae.

I put my phone down on the bench smiling, and Knox hands me the thermometer whilst he's trying to calm the dog down, letting him sniff his hand.

"Who were you texting?" he asks, a wary smile curving his lips.

"Just Braeden," I reply, reassuringly. "He says hello."

Knox's demeanour changes, knowing I was speaking to my brother, and not another guy. We're married, and couldn't be happier, but sometimes Knox still gets a little worried that I'm going to go for a guy closer to my age. It's not going to happen though. I love him with all my heart, and I know he feels the same about me.

"He settling in ok?" Knox asks.

Caz May

"Yeah," I reply, gripping the thermometer tightly. "He's happy, and I'm glad about that."

"Good to hear," Knox replies with a nod. "But time to focus on work now, kitten."

"Yes boss," I reply with a teasing laugh, giving him a quick kiss.

"I love you, Dr Ellersan," I tell him, with a wide smile.

He playfully smacks my butt, teasing me with raspy words, "I love you too, but we can play later, Nurse Ellersan."

We continue to treat the dog then, smiling at each other. And there's honestly nowhere else I'd rather be.

I let Knox Ellersan take my heart and that was the best choice I've made, because our life together is only just beginning.

Take My Heart

Australian Slang Glossary

Ute-Truck

Bludger- someone lazy, doesn't do much and possibly relies on social security benefits

Ripper- something really good/great

Ridgy-Didge- Cool

Bonzer-Great, awesome

Pash/ing/ed- to kiss/make out

Arvo- afternoon

Chunder- Vomit, throw up

Gobby- Blowjob

Aussie Kiss- going down on a girl

Daks- pants/trousers/underwear

Undies/Knickers/Jocks-underwear (female knickers, male Jocks, undies both)

Dakking/ed- to pull or have pulled someone daks down (see above)

Bathers- universal name for female swimwear

Budgie Smugglers- small male swimmer that looks like underwear (google this one to see)

Thongs- Footwear, otherwise known as flip flops

Esky- Cooler-you keep drinks cool in it

Dunny- toilet

Bogan-white trash/trailer trash

Old Fella- Your father/Dad

Franger- Condom, Trojan etc

Caz May

Milo- a malt chocolate powered drink mix (can be made hot or cold)

Macca's-MacDonalds

Fair Dinkum- used to emphasise or seek confirmation of the genuineness or truth of something

Fucking/Bloody oath- similar to above, but an extreme or emphasised way of saying yes.

Shark Week/Rags- A woman's monthly cycle

Stuffed if I know- a nicer way to say fucked if I know

AFL- Australian Rules Football

Giving me a view of her breakfast-

Take My Heart

About the Author

Caz May is a librarian/teacher by trade, but was always destined to be an author from a young age.

In her spare time, she can be found devouring books or writing her own stories with characters that may not be the typical romance heroes but are loveable just as much.

Caz is married to her own real-life bearded hero and has two fur babies.

She lives for Iced coffee, especially from Gloria Jeans or a Farmers Union but pretty much just loves food in general.

When she's not writing, or reading a book most likely she can probably be found asleep or binge-watching shows on Netflix and Stan. And probably also drooling over her character inspiration on Instagram as well.

Check out her Instagram or other socials to get in touch.

Instagram- @cazmayauthor

TikTok- tiktok.com/@cazmayauthor

Facebook- @CazMayAuthor

pinterest-pinterest.com/cazmayauthor

BookBub-Caz May https://www.bookbub.com/profile/caz-may

Spotify- cazcat25

Website- https://cazcat25.wixsite.com/cazmay-author

Goodreads https://www.goodreads.com/cazmay

Caz May

Acknowledgments

Again, the end of another book is here!
I want to say thank you to all of my readers, and
anyone who has encouraged me with this story.
I really struggled with writing this one so getting to this
point with support has been great.
Until the next book,
Caz May xx

Take My Heart

311   **Caz May**

www.ingramcontent.com/pod-product-compliance
Lightning Source LLC
Chambersburg PA
CBHW021313250626
47155CB00002B/521